THREE WEEK

BY
ELINOR GLYN
Author of "The Visits of Elizabeth"

NEW YORK
THE MACAULAY COMPANY
1909

INTRODUCTION TO MY AMERICAN READERS

I feel now, when my "Three Weeks" is to be launched in a new land, where I have many sympathetic friends, that, owing to the misunderstanding and misrepresentation it received from nearly the entire press and a section of the public in England, I would like to state my view of its meaning. (As I wrote it, I suppose it could be believed I know something about that!) For me "the Lady" was a deep study, the analysis of a strange Slav nature, who, from circumstances and education and her general view of life, was beyond the ordinary laws of morality. If I were making the study of a Tiger, I would not give it the attributes of a spaniel, because the public, and I myself, might prefer a spaniel! I would still seek to portray accurately every minute instinct of that Tiger, to make a living picture. Thus, as you read, I want you to think of her as such a study. A great splendid nature, full of the passionate realisation of primitive instincts, immensely cultivated, polished, blase. You must see

INTRODUCTION

her at Lucerne, obsessed with the knowledge of her horrible life with her brutal, vicious husband, to whom she had been sacrificed for political reasons when almost a child. She suddenly sees this young EngUshman, who comes as an echo of something straight and true in manhood which, in outward appearance at all events, she has met in her youth in the person of his Uncle Hubert. She perceives in him at once the Soul sleeping there; and it produces in her a strong emotion. Then I want you to understand the effect of Love on them both. In her it rose from caprice to intense devotion, until the day at the Farm when it reached the highest point—a desire to reproduce his likeness. How, with the most passionate physical emotion, her mental influence upon Paul was ever to raise him to vast aims and noble desires for future greatness. In him love opened the windows of his Soul, so that he saw the -fine in everything.

The immense rush of passion in Venice came frgm her knowledge that they soon must part. Notice the effect of the two griefs on Paul. The first, with its undefined hope, making him do well in all things—even his prowess as a hunter—^to raise himself to be more worthy In her eyes; the second and

INTRODUCTION

paralysing one of death, turning him into adamant until his soul awakens again with the returning spring of her spirit in his heart, and the consolation of the living essence of their love in the child.

The minds of some human beings are as moles, grubbing in the earth for worms. They have no eyes to see God's sky with the stars in it. To such 'Three Weeks' will be but a sensual record of passion. But those who do look up beyond the material will understand the deep pure love, and the Soul in it all, and they will realise that to such a nature as "the Lady's," passion would never have run riot until it was sated—she would have daily grown nobler in her desire to make her Loved One's son a splendid man.

And to all who read, I say—at least be just! and do not skip. No line is written without its having a bearing upon the next, and in its small scope helping to make the presentment of these two human beings vivid and clear.

The verdict I must leave to the Public, but now, at all events,you know,kind Reader,that to me^the "Imperatorskoye" appears a noble woman, because she was absolutely faithful to the man she had selected as her mate, through the one motive which makes a union moral in ethics—

Love.— Elinor Glyn.

THREE WEEKS

CAPTER I

OW this is an episode in a young man's life, and has no real beginning or ending. And you who are old and have forgotten the passions of youth may condemn it. But there are others who ai*e neither old nor young who, perhaps, will understand and find some interest in the study of a strange woman who made the illumination of a brief space.

Paul Verdayne was young and fresh and foolish when his episode began. He believed in himself—he believed in his mother, and in a number of other worthy things. Life was full of certainties for him. He was certain he liked hunting better than anything else in the world— for instance. He was certain he knew his own mmd, and therefore perfectly certain his passion

S

for Isabella Waring would last for ever! Ready to swear eternal devotion with that delightful inconsequence of youth in its unreason, thinking to control an emotion as Canute's flatterers would have had him do the waves.

And the Creator of waves—and emotions— no doubt smiled to Himself—if He is not tired by now of smiling at the follies of the moles called human beings, who for the most part inhabit His earth!

Paul was young, as I said, and fair and strong. He had been in the eleven at Eton and left Oxford with a record for all that should turn a beautiful Englishman into a perfect athlete. Books had not worried him much: The fit of a hunting-coat, the pace of a horse, were things of more importance, but he scraped through his "Smalls" and his "Mods," and was considered by his friends to be anything but a fool. As for his mother—the Lady Henrietta Verdayne—she thought him a god among men!

Paul went to London like others of his time, and attended the theatres, where perfectly virtuous young ladies display nightly their innocent charms in hilarious choruses, arrayed in the latest

modes. He supped, too, with these houris— and felt himself a man of the world.

He had stayed about in country houses for perhaps a year, and had danced through the whole of a season with all the prettiest dehi^ tantes. And one or two of the young married women of forty had already marked him out for their prey.

By all this you can see just the kind of creature Paul was. There are hundreds of others like him, and perhaps they, too, have the latent qualities which he developed during his episode— only they remain as he was in the beginning—sound -asleep.

That fall out hunting in March, and being laid up with a sprained ankle and a broken collarbone, proved the commencement of the Isabella Waring affair.

She was the parson's daughter—and is still for the matter of that!—and often in those days between her games of golf and hockey, or a good run on her feet with the hounds, she came up to Verdayne Place to write Lady Henrietta's letters for her. Isabella was most amiable and delighted to make herself useful.

And if her hands were big and re9, she wrote clearly and well. The Lady Henrietta, who herself was of the delicate Later Victorian Dresden China type, could not imagine a state of things which contained the fact that her god-like son might stoop to this daughter of the earthy earth!

Yet so it fell about. Isabella read aloud the sporting papers to him—Isabella played piquet with him in the dull late afternoons of his convalescence—Isabella herself washed his dog Pike —that king of rough terriers! And one terrible day Paul unfortunately kissed the large pink lips of Isabella as his mother entered the room. , I will draw a veil over this part of his life.

The Lady Henrietta, being a great lady, chanced to behave as such on the occasion referred to—but she was also a woman, and not a particularly clever one. Thus Paul was soon irritated by opposition into thinking himself seriously in love with this daughter of the middle classes, so far beneath his noble station.

"Let the boy have his fling," sard Sir Charles Verdayne, who was a coarse person. "Damn it all! a man is not obliged to marry every woman he kisses!"

"A gentlemen does not deliberately kiss an unmarried girl unless he intends to make her his wife!" retorted Lady Henrietta. "I fear the worst 1"

Sir Charles snorted and chuckled, two unpleasant and annoying habits his lady wife had never been able to break him of. So the affair grew and grew! Until towards the middle of April Paul was advised to travel for his health.

"Your father and I can sanction no engagement, Paul, before you return," said Lady Henrietta. "If, in July, on your twenty-third birthday, you still wish to break your mother's heart —I suppose you must do so. But I ask of you the unfettered reflection of three months first."

This seemed reasonable enough, and Paul consented to start upon a tour round Europe— ^not having spoken the final fatal and binding words to Isabella Waring. They made their adieux in the pouring rain under a dripping oak in the lane by the Vicarage gate.

Paul was six foot two, and Isabella quite six foot, and broad in proportion. They were pressed aln^ost §like, and at a little distance, but

for the lady's scanty petticoat, it would have been difficult to distinguish her sex.

"Good-bye, old chap," she said "We have been real pals, and I'll not forget you!"

But Paul, who was feeling sentimental, put it differently.

"Good-bye, darling," he whispered witH a suspicion of tremble in his charming voice. "I shall never love any woman but you^—never, never in my life."

Cuckoo! screamed the bird in the tree.

And now we are getting nearer the episode. Paris bored Paul—^he did not know its joys and was in no mood to learn them. He mooned about and went to the races. His French was too indifferent to make theatres a pleasure, and the attractive ladies who smiled at his blue eyes were for him defendues. A man so recently parted from the only woman he could ever love had no •right to look at such things, he thought. How young and chivalrous and honest he was—^poor Paul!

So he took to visiting Versailles and Fontaine-bleau and Compiegne with a guide-book, and came to the conclusion it was all "beastly rot."

So he turned his back upon France and fled to Switzerland.

Do you know Switzerland?—^you who read. Do you know it at the beginning of May? A feast of blue lakes, and snow-peaks, and the divinest green of young beeches, and the sombre shadow of dark firs, and the exhilaration of the air.

If you do, I need not tell you about it. Only in any case now, you must see it through the eyes of Paul. That is if you intend to read another page of this bad book.

It was pouring with rain when he drove from the station to the hotel. His temper was at its worst. Pilatus hid his head in mist, the Biirgen-stock was invisible—it was chilly, too, and the fire smoked in the sitting-room when Paul had it lighted.

His heart yearned for his own snug room at Verdayne Place, and the jolly voice of Isabella Waring counting point, quint and quatorze. What nonsense to send him abroad. As if such treatment could be effectual as a cure for a loye like his. He almost laughed at his mother's folly. How he longed to sit down and write to

his Sarllng-. Write and tell how he hated it all, and was only getting through the time until he saw her six feet of buxom charms again—only-Paul did not put it like that—indeed, he never thought about her charms at all—or want of them. He analysed nothing. He was sound asleep, you see, to nuances as yet; he was just a splendid English young animal of the best class.

He had promised not to write to Isabella— or, if he must, at least not to write a love-letter.

"Dear boy," the Lady Henrietta had said when giving him her fond parting kiss, "if you are very unhappy and feel you greatly wish to write to Miss Waring, I suppose you must do so, but let your letter be about the scenery and the impressions of travel, in no way to be interpreted into a declaration of affection or a promise of future union—I have your word, Paul, for that?"

And Paul had given his word.

"All right, mother—I promise—for three months."

And now on this wet evening the "must" had come, so he pulled out some hotel paper and began.

"My Dear Isabella:

"I say—^you know—I hate beginning like this— I have arrived at this beastly place, and I am awfully unhappy. I think it would have been better if I had brought Pike with me, only those rotten laws about getting the little chap back to England would have been hard. How is Moonlighter? And have they really looked after that strain, do you gather? Make Trem-lett come down and report progress to you daily —I told him to. My rooms look out on a beastly lake, and there are mountains, I suppose, but I can't see them. There is hardly any one in the hotel, because the Easter visitors have all g'one back and the summer ones haven't come, so I doubt even if I can have a game of billiards. I am sick of guide-books, and I should like to take the next train home again. I must dress for dinner now, and I'll finish this to-night."

Paul dressed for dinner; his temper was vile, and his valet trembled. Then he went down into the restaurant scowling, and was ungracious to the polite and conciliating waiters, ordering his food and a bottle of claret as if they had done

him an injury. '^Anglais," they said to one another behind the serving-screen, pointing their thumbs at him—"he pay but he damn.'*

Then Paul sent for the New York Herald and propped it up in front of him, prodding at some ohves with his fork, one occasionally reaching his mouth, while he read, and awaited his soup.

The table next to him in this quiet corner was laid for one, and had a bunch of roses in the centre, just two or three exquisite blooms that he was familiar with the appearance of in the Paris shops. Nearly all the other tables were empty or emptying; he had dined very late. Who could want roses eating alone ? The menu, too, was written out and ready, and an expression of expectancy lightened the face of the head waiter—^who himself brought a bottle of most carefully decanted red wine, feeling the temperature through the fine glass with the air of a great connoisseur.

"One of those over-fed foreign brutes of no sex, I suppose," Paul said to himself, and turned to the sporting notes in front of him.

He did not look up again until he heard the rustle of a dress.

THREE WEEKS

The woman had to pass him—even so close that the heavy silk touched his foot. He fancied he smelt tuberoses, but it was not until she sat down, and he again looked at her, that he perceived a knot of them tucked into the front of her bodice.

K woman to order dinner for herself beforehand, and have special wine and special roses— special attention, too! It was simply disgusting!

Paul frowned. He brought his brown eyebrows close together, and glared at the creature with his blue young eyes.

An elderly, dignified servant in black livery stood behind her chair. She herself was all in black, and her hat—an expensive, distinguished-looking hat—cast a shadow over her eyes. He could just see they were cast down on her plate. Her face was white, he saw that plainly enough, startlingly white, like a magnolia bloom, and contained no marked features. No' features at all! he said to himself. Yes—he was wrong, she had certainly a mouth worth looking at again. It was so red. Not large and pink and laughingly open like Isabella's, but straight and chiselled, and red, red, red.

THREE WEEKS

Paul was young, but he knew paint when fie saw it, and this red was real, and vivid, and disconcerted him.

He began his soup—hers came at the same time; she had only toyed with some caviare by way of hors d'oouvre, and it angered him to notice the obsequiousness of the waiters, who passed each thing to the dignified serv^ant to be placed before the lady by his hand. Who was she to be served with this respect and rapidity?

Only her red wine the maitre d'hotel poured into her glass himself. She lifted it up to the light to see the clear ruby, then she sipped it and scented its bouquet, the mattre d'hotel anxiously awaiting her verdict the while. ^^Bon" was all she said, and the weight of the world seemed to fall from the man's sloping shoulders as he bowed and moved aside.

Paul's irritation grew. "She's well over thirty," he said to himself. "I suppose she has nothing else to live for! I wonder what the devil she'll eat next!"

She ate a delicate truite bleu, but she did not touch her wine again the while. She had almost finished the fish before Paul's sole au vin hlanc

THREE WEEKS

arrived upon the scene, and this angered him the more. Why should he wait for his dinner while this woman feasted? Why, indeed. What would her next course be? He found himself unpleasantly interested to know. The tenderest selle d'agneau au lait and the youngest green peas made their appearance, and again the maitre d'hotel returned, having mixed the salad.

Paul noticed with all these things the lady ate but a small portion of each. And it was not until a fat quail arrived later, while he himself was trying to get through two mutton chops a ranglaise, that she again tasted her claret. Yes, it was claret, he felt sure, and probably wonderful claret at that. Confound her! Paul turned to the wine list. What could it be? Chateau Latour at fifteen francs? Chateau Mar-gaux, or Cliateau Lafite at twenty?—or possibly it was not here at all, and was special, too— like the roses and the attention. He called his waiter and ordered some port—lie felt he could not drink another drop of his modest St. Estephe!

All this time the lady had never once looked at him; indeed, except that one occasion when she had lifted her head to examine the wine with

THREE WEEKS

the light through it, he had not seen her raise her eyes, and then the glass had been between himself and her. The white lids with their heavy lashes began to irritate him. What colour could they be? those eyes underneath. They were not very large, that was certain— ^probably black, too, like her hair. Little black eyes! That was ugly enough, surely! And he hated heavy black hair growing in those unusual great waves. Women's hair should be light and fluffy and fuzzy, and kept tidy in a net—like Isabella*s. This looked so thick—enough to strangle one, if she twisted it round one's throat. What strange ideas were those coming into his head? Why should she think of twisting her hair round a man's throat? It must be the port mounting to his brain, he decided—he was not given to speculating in this way about women.

What would she eat next? And why did it interest him what she ate or did not eat? The maitre d'hote! again appeared with a dish of marvellous-looking nectarines. The waiter now handed the dignified servant the finger-bowl, into which he poured rose-water. Paul could just distinguish ihe scent of it, and then he noticed

THREE V/EEKS

the lady's hands. Yes, they at least were faultless; he could not cavil at them; slender and white, with that transparent whiteness like mother-of-pearl. And what pink nails! And how polished! Isabella's hands—but he refused to think of them.

By this time he was conscious of an absorbing interest thrilling his whole being— disapproving irritated interest.

The maitre d'hotel now removed the claret, out of which the lady had only drunk one glass.

(What waste! thought Paul.)

And then he returned with a strange-looking bottle, and this time the dignified servant poured the brilliant golden fluid into a tiny liqueur-glass. What could it be ? Paul was familiar with most liqueurs. Had he not dined at every restaurant in London, and supped with houris who adored creme de menthef But this was none he knew. He had heard of Tokay—Imperial Tokay—could it be that ? And where did she get it ? And who the devil was the woman, anyway?

She peeled the nectarine leisurely—she seemed to enjoy it more than all the rest of her dinner. And what could that expression mean on her

THREE WEEKS

face? Inscrutable—cynical was it? No—absorbed. As absolutely unconscious of self and others as if she had been alone in the room. What could she be thinking of never to worry to look about her?

He began now to notice her throat, it was rounded and intensely white, through the transparent black stuff. She had no strings of pearls or jewels on—^unless—^yes, that was a great sapphire gleaming from the folds of gauze on her neck. Not surrounded by diamonds like ordinary brooches, but just a big single stone so dark and splendid it seemed almost black. There was another on her hand, and yet others in her ears.

Her ears were not anything so very wonderful! Not so very! Isabella's were quite as good— and this thought comforted him a little. As far as he could see beyond the roses and the table she was a slender woman, and he had not noticed on her entrance if she were tall or short. He could not say why he felt she must be well over thirty—there was not a line or wrinkle on her face—not even the slight nip in under the chin, or the tell-tale strain beside the ears.

She was certainly not pretty, certainly not.

THREE WEEKS

Well shaped—yes—and graceful as far as Ke could judge; but pretty—a thousand times No!

Then the speculation as to her nationality began. French? assuredly not. English? ridiculous! Equally so German. Italian? perhaps. Russian? possibly. Hungarian? probably.

Paul had drunk his third glass of port and was beginning his fourth. This was far more than his usual limit. Paul was, as a rule, an abstemious young man. Why he should have deliberately sat and drank that night he never knew. His dinner had been moderate—distinctly moderate—and he had watched a refined feast of Lucullus partaken of by a woman who only tasted each plat!

T wonder what she will have to pay for it all ?' he thought to himself. "She will probably sign the bill, though, and I shan't see."

But when the lady had finished her nectarine and dipped her slender fingers in the rose-water she got up—she had not smoked, she could not be Russian then. Got up and walked towards the door, signing no bill, and paying no gold.

Paul stared as she passed him—rudely stared —he knew it afterwards and felt ashamed. How-

THREE WEEKS

ever, the lady never so much as noticed him, nor did she raise her eyes, so that when she had finally disappeared he was still unaware of their colour or expression.

But what a figure she had! Sinuous, supple, rounded, and yet very slight.

"She must have the smallest possible bones," Paul said to himself, "because it looks all curvy and soft, and yet she is as slender as a gazelle."

She was tall, too, though not six feet—like Isabella!

The waiters and maitre d'hotel all bowed and stood aside as she left, followed by her elderly, stately, silver-haired servant.

Of course it would have been an easy matter to Paul to find out her name, and all about her. He would only have had to summon Monsieur Jacques, and ask any question he pleased. But for some unexplained reason he would not do this. Instead of which he scowled in front of him, and finished his fourth glass of port. Then his head swam a little, and he went outside into the night. The rain had stopped and the sky was full of stars scattered in its intense blue. It was warm, too, there, under the clipped trees, SSaxil

THREE WEEKS

hoped he wasn't drunk—such a beastly thing to do! And not even good port either.

He sat on a bench and smoked a cigar. A strange sense of lonehness came over him. It seemed as if he were far, far away from any one in the world he had ever known. A vague feeling of oppression and coming calamity passed through him, only he was really as yet too material and thoroughly, solidly English to entertain it, or any other subtle mental emotion for more than a minute. But he undoubtedly felt strange to-night; different from what he had ever done before. He would have said "weird" if he could have thought of the word. The woman and her sinuous, sensuous black shape filled the space of his mental vision. Black hair, black hat, black dress—and of course black eyes. Ah! if he could only know their colour really!

iThe damp bench where he sat was just under the ivy hanging from the balustrade of the small terrace belonging to the ground-floor suite at the end.

There was a silence, very few people passed, frightened no doubt by the recent rain. He seemed alone in the world.

The wine now began to fire his senses. Why should he remain alone? He was young and rich and—surely even in Lucerne there must be—. And then he felt a beast, and looked out on to the lake.

Suddenly his heart seemed to swell with some emotion, a faint scent of tuberoses filled the air —and from exactly above his head there came a gentle, tender sigh.

He started violently, and brusquely turned and looked up. Almost indistinguishable in the deep shadow he saw the woman's face. It seemed to emerge from a mist of black gauze. And looking down into his were a pair of eyes—a pair of eyes. For a moment Paul's heart felt as if it had stopped beating, so wonderful was their effect upon him. They seemed to draw him—draw something out of him—intoxicate him—paralyse him. And as he gazed up motionless the woman moved noiselessly back on to the terrace, and he saw nothing but the night sky studded with stars.

Had he been dreaming? Had she really bent over the ivy? Was he mad? Yes—or drunk, because now he had seen the eyes, and yet he did not know their colour! Were they black, or

blue, or grey, or green? He did not know, he could not think—only they were eyes— eyes— eyes.

The letter to Isabella Waring remained unfinished that night.

?s

CHAPTER II

PAUL'S Head acHed a good deal next morning and he was disinclined to rise. However, the sun blazed in at his windows, and a bird sang in a tree.

His temper was the temper of next day—sodden, and sullen, and ashamed. He even resented the sunshine.

But what a beautiful creature he looked, as later he stepped into a boat for a row on the lake! His mother, the Lady Henrietta, had truly reason to be proud of him. So tall and straight, and fair and strong. And at the risk of causing a second fit among some of the critics, I must add, he probably wore silk socks, and was "beautifully groomed," too, as all young Englishmen are of his class and age. And how supple his lithe body seemed as he bent over the oars, while the boat shot out into the blue water.

The mountains were really very jolly, he

thought, and it was not too hot, and he was glad he had come out, even though he had eaten no breakfast and was feeHng rather cheap still. Yes, very glad.

After he had advanced a few hundred yards he rested on his oars, and looked up at the hotel. Then wonder came back to him, where was she to-day—^the lady with the eyes? Or had he dreamed it—and was there no lady at all?

It should not worry him anyway—so he rowed ahead, and ceased to speculate.

The first thing he did when he came in for lunch was to finish his letter to Isabella.

"P. S.—Monday," he added. "It is finer today, and I have had some exercise. The view isn't bad now the mist has gone. I shall do some climbing, I think. Take care of yourself, dear girl. Good-bye.

"Love from

"Paul."

It was with a feeling of excitement that he entered the restaurant for dejeuner. Would she be there? How would she seem in daylight?

But the little table where she had sat the night

THREE WEEKS

before was uncx:cupied. There were the usual cloth and glass and silver, but no preparations for any specially expected guest upon it. Paul felt annoyed with himself because his heart sank. Had she gone? Or did she only dine in public? Perhaps she lunched in the sitting-room beyond the terrace, where he had seen her eyes the night before.

The food was really very good, and the sun shone, and Paul was young and hungry, so presently he forgot about the lady and enjoyed his meal.

The appearance of the Biirgenstock across the lake attracted him, as afterwards he smoked another cigar under the trees. He would hire an electric launch and go there and explore the paths. If only Pike were with him—or—Isabella!

This idea he put into execution.

What a thing was a funicular railway. How steep and unpleasant, but how quaint the tree-tops looked when one was up among them. Yes —Lucerne was a good deal jollier than Paris. And he roamed about among the trees, never noticing their beautiful colours. Presently he paused to rest, He was soothed—^ven peaceful

THREE WEEKS

If he had Pike he could really be quite happy, He thought.

What was that rustle among the leaves above him ? He looked up, and started then as violently almost as he had done the night before. Because there, peeping at him from the tender green of the young beeches, was the lady in black. She looked down upon him through the parted boughs, her black hat and long black veil making a sharp silhouette against the vivid verdure, her whole face in tender shadow and framed in tht misty gauze.

Paul's heart beat violently. He felt a pulse in his throat—for a few seconds.

He knew he was gazing into her eyes, and he thought he knew they were green. They looked larger than he had imagined them to be. They were set so beautifully, too, just a suspicion of rise at the corners. And their expression was mocking and compelling—and— But she let go the branches and disappeared from view.

Paul stood still. He was thrilling all over. Should he bound in among the trees and follow; her? Should he call out and ask her to come back? Should he—? But when he had decided

THREE WEEKS

and gained the spot where she must have stood, he saw it was a junction of three paths, and he was in perfect ignorance which one she had taken. He rushed down the first of them, but it twisted and turned, and when he had gone far enough to see ahead—there was no one in sight. So he retraced his steps and tried the second. This, too, ended in disappointment. And the third led to an opening where he could see the descending funiadaire, and just as it sank out of view he caught sight of a black dress, almost hidden by a standing man's figure, whom he recognised as the elderly silver-haired servant.

Paul had learnt a number of swear-words at Eton and Oxford. And he let the trees hear most of them then.

He could not get down himself until the train returned, and by that time where would she be? To go by the paths would take an eternity. This time circumstance had fairly done him.

Presently he sauntered back to the little hotel whose terrace commands the lake far below, and eagerly watching the craft upon it, he thought he caught sight of a black figure reclining in an electric launch which sped over the blue water.

Then he began to reason with himself. Wfij; should the sight of this woman have caused him such violent emotion? Why? Women were jolly things that did not matter much—except Isabella. She mattered, of course, but somehow her mental picture came less readily to his mind than usual. The things he seemed to see most distinctly were her hands—her big red hands. And then he unconsciously drifted from all thought of her.

"She certainly looks younger in daylight," he said to himself. "Not more than thirty perhaps. And what strange hats with that shadow over her eyes. What is she doing here all alone? She must be somebody from the people in the hotel making such a fuss —and that servant— Then why alone?'* He mused and mused.

She was not a demi-mondaine. The English ones he knew were very ordinary people, but he had heard of some of the French ladies as being quite grande dame, and travelling en prince. Yet he was convinced this was not one of them. Who could she be? He must know.

To go back to the hotel would be the shortest

way to find out, and so by the next descending train he left the Biirg-enstock.

He walked up and down under the lime-trees outside the terrace of her rooms for half an hour, but was not rewarded in any way for his pains. And at last he went in. He, too, would have a clinner worth eating, he thought. So he consulted the maitre d'hotel on his way up to dress, and together they evolved a banquet. Paul longed to question the man about the unknown, but as yet he was no actor, and he found he felt too much about it to do it naturally, i He dressed with the greatest care, and descended at exactly half-past eight. Yes, the table was laid for her evidently— ^but there were giant carnations, not roses, in the silver vase to-night. How quickly the waiters seemed to bring things! And what a frightful lot there was to eat! And •dawdle as he would, by nine o'clock he had almost finished. Perhaps it would be as well to send 'for a newspaper again. Anything to delay his 'Having to rise and go out. An anxious, uncomfortable gnawing sense of expectancy dominated him. How ridiculous for a woman to be so late! SYbat cook could do justice to his dishes if thejr

were thus to be kept waiting? She couldn't possibly have ordered it for half past nine, surely! Gradually, as that hour passed and his second cup of coffee had been sipped to its finish, Paul felt a sickening sense of anger and disappointment. He got up abruptly and went out. In the hall, coming from the corridor of her rooms, he met the lady face to face.

Then rage with himself seized him. Why had he not waited? For no possible reason could he go back now. And what a chance to look at her missed—and all thrown away.

He sat sullenly down in the hall, resisting the temptation to go into the beautiful night. At least he would see her on her way back. But he waited until nearly eleven, and she never appeared, and then the maddening thought came to him—she had probably passed to her rooms along the terrace outside, under the lime-tree.

He bounded up, and stalked into the starlight. He could see through the windows of the restaurant, and no one was there. Then he sat on the bench again, under the ivy—but all was darkness and silence; and thoroughly depressed, Paul at last went to bed.

Next day was so gloriously fine that youth and health sang within him. He was up and away quite early. Not a thought of this strange lady should cross his mind for the entire day, he determined as he ate his breakfast. And soon he started for the Rigi in a launch, taking the English papers with him. Intense joy, too! A letter from Isabella!

Such a nice letter. All about Pike and Moonlighter, and the other horses—and Isabella was going to stay with a friend at Blackheath, where she hoped to get better golf than at home—and Lady Henrietta had been gracious to her, and given her Paul's address, and there had been a "jolly big party" at Verdayne Place for Sunday, but none of his "pals." At least if there were, they were not in church, she added naively.

All this Paul read in his launch on the way to the Rigi, and for some unexplained reason the information seemed about things a long way off, and less thrilling than usual. He had a splendid climb, and when he got back to Lucerne in the evening he was thoroughly tired, and so hungry he flew down to his dinner.

It was nearly nine o'clock; at least if she came

to-night he would be there to see her. But of course it did not matter if she came or not, he had conquered that ridiculous interest. He would hardly look until he reached his table. Yes, there she was, but dipping her white fingers in the rose-water at the very end of her repast.

And again, in spite of himself, a strange wild thrill ran through Paul, and he knew it was what he had been subconsciously hoping for all day —and oh, alas! it mattered exceedingly.

The lady never glanced at him. She swept from the room, her stately graceful movements delighting his eye. He could understand and appreciate movement—was he not accustomed to thoroughbreds, and able to judge of their action and line?

How blank the space seemed when she had gone—dull and unspeakably uninteresting. He became impatient with the slowness of the waiters, who had seemed to hurry unnecessarily the night before. But at last his meal ended, and he went out under the trees. The sky was so full of stars it hardly seemed dark. The air was soft, and in the distance a band played a plaintive valse tune.

There were numbers of people walking about, and the lights from the hotel windows lit up the scene. Only the ivy terrace was in shadow as he again sat down on the bench.

How had she got in last night? That he must find out—he rose, and peered about him. Yes, there was a little gate, a flight of steps, a private entrance into this suite, just round the corner.

And as he looked at it, the lady, wrapped in a scarf of black gauze, passed him, and standing aside while the silver-haired servant opened the little door with a key, she then entered and disappeared from view.

It seemed as if the stars danced to Paul. His whole being was quivering with excitement, and now he sat on the bench again almost trembling.

He did not move for at least half an hour; then the clocks chimed in the town. No, there was no hope; he would see her no more that night. He rose listlessly to go back to bed, tired out with his day's climb. And as he stood up, there, above the ivy again, he saw her face looking down upon him.

How had she crossed the terrace without his hearing her? How long had she been there?

But what matter ? At least she was there. ^KxA those eyes looking into his out of the shadow, what did they say? Surely they smiled at him. Paul jumped on to the bench. Now he was almost level with her face—almost—and his was raised eagerly in expectation. Was he dreaming, or did she whisper something? The sound was so soft he was not quite sure. He stretched out his arms to her in the darkness, pulling himself by the ivy nearer still. And this time there was no mistake.

"Come, Paul," she said. "I have some words to say to you."

And round to the little gate Paul flew.

CHAPTER III

PAUL was never quite sure of what hap pened that evening—everything was so wonderful, so unusual, so unlike his ordinary life. The gate was unlocked he found when he got there, but no one appeared to be inside, and he bounded up the steps and on to the terrace. Silence and darkness—^was she fooling him then? No, there she was by one of the windows; he could dimly see her outline as she passed into the room beyond, through some heavy curtains. That was why no light came through to the terrace. He followed, dropping them after him also, and then he found himself in a room as unlike a hotel as he could imagine. It may have had the usual brocade walls and gilt chairs of the "best suite," but its aspect was so transformed by her subtle taste and presence, it seemed to him unique, and there were masses of flowers—roses, big white ones—tuberoses—lilies of the valley, gardenias, late violets. The lights

were low and shaded, and a great couch filled one side of the room beyond the fireplace. Such a couch! covered with a tiger-skin and piled with pillows, all shades of rich purple velvet and silk, embroidered with silver and gold—unlike any pillows he had ever seen before, even to their shapes. The whole thing was different and strange—and intoxicating.

The lady had reached the couch, and sank into it. She was in black still, but gauzy, clinging black, which seemed to give some gleam of purple underneath. And if he had not been sure that in daylight he had thought they were green, he would have sworn the eyes which now looked into his were deepest violet, too.

"Come," she said. "You may sit here beside me and tell me what you think."

And her voice was like rich music—^but she had hardly any accent. She might have been an Englishwoman almost, for that matter, and yet he somehow knew that she was not. Perhaps it was she pronounced each word; nothing was slurred over. Without her hat she looked even more attractive, and certainly younger. But what was age or youth? And what was beauty

itself, when a woman whose face was neither young nor beautiful could make him feel he was looking" at a divine goddess, and thrilling as he had never dreamt of doing in his short life?

If any one had told Paul this was going- to happen to him, this experience, he would have laughed them to scorn. To begin with, he was rather shy with ladies as a rule, and had not learnt a trick of entreprenance. It took him quite a while to know one well enough to even talk at ease. And yet here he was, embarked upon an adventure which savoured of the Arabian Nights.

He came forward and sat down, and he could feel the pulse beating in his throat. It all seemed perfectly natural at the time, but afterwards he wondered how she had known his name was Paul —and how it had all come to pass.

"For three days you have thought of me, Paul —-is it not so?" she said, half closing her lids.

But he could only blurt out "Yes!" while he devoured her with his eyes.

"We are both—how shall I say—drifting— holiday-making—trying to forget. And we must talk a little together, n'est-ce pas? Tell

"Oh', yes!" said Paul.

*'You are beautiful, you know, Paul," she went on. "So tall and straight like you English, with curly hair of gold. Your mother must have loved you as a baby."

"I suppose she did," said Paul. ' **She is well ? Your mother, the stately lady ?"

*'Very well—do you know her ?" he asked, surprised.

"Long ago I have seen her, and I knew you at once, so like you are—and to your uncles, especially the Lord Hubert."

"Uncle Hubert is a rotter!"

"A—rotter?" inquired the lady. "And what is that ?" And she smiled a divine smile.

Paul felt ashamed. "Oh! well, it is a rotter, you know—that is—like Uncle Hubert, I mean."

She laughed again. "You do not explain well, but I understand you. And so you only resemble the Uncle Hubert on the outside—that is good."

Paul felt jealous. Lord Hubert Aldringham's reputation—for some things—was European. "I hope so," he said with emphasis. "And you knew him well then, too ?"

"I never said so," replied the ladjr. "I saw

him once—twice perhaps—years ago—at tHe marriage of a princess. There, it has made you frown, we will speak no more of the Uncle Hubert !" and she leant back and laughed.

Paul felt very young. He wanted to show her he was grown up, and he wanted a number of things which had never even formed themselves in his imagination before. But she went on talking.

"And your cotelettes were tough, Paul, and you were so cross that first evening, and hated me! And oh! Paul, you had far too much wine for a boy like you!"

He reddened to the roots of his fair wavy hair, and then he hung his head.

"I know I did—it was beastly of me—^but I was so—upset—I—"

"Look at me," she said, and she bent forward over him—a gliding feline movement infinitely sinuous and attractive.

Then he looked, his big blue eyes still cloudy with a mist of shame.

"You must tell me why you were upset, baby —Paul!"

How often she said his name! lingering over it as if it were music. It thrilled him every time.

Then he gained courage.

"But how did you know anything about it—or what I had—or what I drank ? You never once raised your eyehds all the time!"

"Perhaps I can see through them when I want to—who knows!" and she laughed.

"And you wanted to—wanted to see through them?"

He was gazing at her now, and she suddenly looked down, while the most beautiful transparent pink flushed her soft white cheeks, turning her into a tender girl almost. The change was so sudden, it startled Paul, and emboldened him.

"You wanted to!" he repeated in a glad voice. "You wanted to see me?"

"Yes," she whispered, and she looked up at him, but this time there was mischief in her eyes.

"Is that why you sighed then among the ivy? What made you sigh ?"

She paused a moment, and then she said slowly: "A number of things. You seemed so young, and so beautiful, and so—asleep."

"Indeed I wasn't asleep!" Paul exclaimed. "It would take a great deal more port than that to make me go to sleep. I was thinking of—" And

THREE WEEKS

then he saw she had not meant that kind of sleep, and felt a fool—and wondered.

She helped him out.

"All this time you have not told me why you were upset—upset enough to drink bad port. That was naughty of you, Paul."

"I was upset—over you. I was angry because I was so interested—" and he reddened again.

She leant back among the purple cushions, her figure so supple in its lines, it made him think of a snake. She half closed her eyes again—^and she spoke low in a dreamy voice:

"It was fate, Paul. I knew it when I entered the room. I felt it again among the green trees, and so I ran from you—^but to-night it is plus fort que mot —so I called you to come in."

"I am so glad—so glad" said Paul.

She remained silent. Her eyes in their narrowed lids gleamed at him, seeming to penetrate into his very soul. And now he noticed her mouth again. It neither drooped nor smiled, it was straight, and chiselled and strong, and small rather, and the lower lip was rounded and slightly cleft in the centre. A most appetising red flower of a mouth.

THREE WEEKS

By this time Paul was more or less intoxicated with excitement, he had lost all sense of time and place. It seemed as if he had known her always —that there never had been a moment when she had not filled the whole of his horizon.

They were both silent for a couple of minutes. As far as he could gather from her inscrutable face, she was weighing things—what things?

Suddenly she sprang up, one of those fine movements of hers full of cat-like grace.

*Taul," she said, "listen," and she spoke rather fast. "You are so young, so young—and I shall hurt you—^probably. Won*t you go now—while there is yet time? Away from Lucerne, back to Paris—even back to England. Anywhere away from me."

She put her hand on his arm, and looked up into his eyes. And there were tears in hers. And now he saw that they were grey.

He was moved as never yet in all his life.

**I will not!" he said. "I may be young, but to-night I know—I want to live! And I will chance the hurt, because I know that onlj YP^ can teach me—^just how—•"

THREE WEEKS

Then his voice broke, and he bent down and covered her hand with kisses.

She quivered a little and drew away. She picked up a great bunch of tuberoses, and broke off all their tops. "There, take them!" she said, pressing them into his hands, and those against his heart. **Take them and go—^and dream of me. You have chosen. Dream of me to-night and remember—^there is to-morrow."

Then she glided back from him, and before he realised it she had gone noiselessly away through another door.

Paul stood still. The room swam; his head swam. Then he stumbled out cwi to the terrace, under the night sky, the white blossoms still pressed against his heart.

He must have walked about for hours. The grey dawn was creeping over the silent world when at last he went back to the hotel and to his bed.

There he slept and dreamt—never a dream! For youth and health are glorious things. And he was tired out.

The great sun was high in the heavens when next he awoke. And the room was full of the

scent of tuberoses, scattered on the pillow beside him. Presently, when his blue eyes began to take in the meaning of things, he remembered and bounded up. For was not this the commencement of his first real day?

CHAPTER IV

[HE problem which faced Paul, wHen he had finished a very late breakfast, was how he should see her soon—^the lady in black.

He could not go and call like an ordinary visitor, because he did not know her name! That was wonderful—did not even know her name, or anything about her, only that his whole being was thrilling with anxiety to see her again.

The simplest thing to do seemed to descend into the hall and look at the Visitors' List, which he promptly did.

There were only a few people in the hotel; it was not hard, therefore, guessing at the numbers of the rooms, to arrive at the conviction that "Mme. Zalenska and suite" might be what he was searching for. Zalenska—she was possibly Russian after all. And what was her christian name? That he longed to know.

As he stood staring, his fair forehead puckered into a frown of thought, the silver-haired servant came up behind him and said, with his respectful, dignified bearing:

"De la part de Madame," handing Paul a letter the while.

What could it contain ?

But this was not the moment for speculation— he would read and see.

He turned his back on the servant, and walked towards the light, while he tore open the envelope. It had the most minute sphinx in the corner, and the paper was un-English, and rather thin.

This was what he read:

'^Morning, "Paul, I am young to-day, and we must see the blue lake and the green trees. Come to the landing towards the station, and I will call for you in my launch. And you shall be young, too, Paul —and teach me! Give Dmitry the answer."

"The answer is, *Yes, immediately'—^tell Madame," Paul said.

And then he trod on air until he arrived at the landing she had indicated. Soon the launch glided up, he saw her there reclining under an awning of striped green.

It was a well-arranged launch, the comfortable deck-chairs were in the bows, and the steering took place from a raised perch behind the cabin, so the two were practically alone. The lady was in grey to-day, and it suited her strangely. Her eyes gleamed at him, full of mischief, under her large grey hat.

Paul drew his chair a little forward, turning it so that he could look at her without restraint.

"How good of you to send for me," he said delightedly.

She smiled a radiant smile. "Was it? I am capricious, I did not think of the good for you, only I wanted you—to please myself. I wish to be foolish to-day, Paul, and see your eyes dance, and watch the light on your curls."

Paul frowned; it was as if she thought him a baby.

Then the lady leant back and laughed, the sound was of golden bells.

'Yes, you are a baby!" she said, answering

50

<r

his thoughts. "A great, big, beautiful baby, Paul."

If Paul had been a girl he would have pouted.

She turned from him and gazed over the lake; it was looking indescribably beautiful, with the colours of the springtime.

"Do 5"ou see the green of those beeches by the water, Paul ? Look at their tenderness, next the dark firs—and then the blue beyond—and see, there is a copper beech, he is king of them all! I would like to build a chalet up in some part like that, and come there each year in May—to read fairy-tales."

For the first time in his life Paul saw with different eyes—just the beauty of things—and forgot to gauge their sporting possibilities. An infinite joy was flooding his being, some sensation he had not dreamed about even, of happiness and fulfilment.

She appeared to him more alluring than ever, and young and gay—as young as Isabella! And then his thoughts caused him to take in his breath with a hiss—Isabella—how far away she seemed. Of course he could never love any one else— but—

SI

"Don't think of it, then,'* the lady whispered. **Be young Hke me, and live under the blue sky."

How was it she knew his thoughts always? He blushed while he stammered: "No—I won't think of it—or an3^thing but you—Princess."

"Daring one!" she said, "who told you to call me that? The hotel people have been talking, I suppose."

"No," said Paul, surprised, "I called you Princess just because you seem like one to me— ^but now I guess from what you say, you are not plain Madame Zaienska."

Her eyes clouded for a second. "Madame Zaienska does to travel with—but you shall call me what you like."

He grew emboldened.

"I suddenly feel I want so much—I want to know why your eyes were so mocking through the trees on the Biirrgenstock? They drove me nearly mad, you know, and I raced about after you like a dog after a hare!"

"I thought you would—^you did not control the expression when you gazed up at me! And so I was the true hare—and ran away!"

She looked down suddenly and was silent for

THREE WEEKS

some moments, then she turned the conversation from these personal things. She led his thoughts into new channels—made him observe the trees and sky, and the v/onderful beauty of it all, and with lightning flashes took him into unknown speculations on emotions and the meaning of things.

A new existence seemed to open to Paul's view. And all the while she lay back in her chair almost motionless, only her wonderful eyes lit up the strange whiteness of her face. There was not a touch of niaiLvaise honte, or explanation of the unusualness of this situation in her manner. It had a perfect, quiet dignity, as if to look into the eyes of an unknown young man at night over an ivy terrace, and then spend a day with him alone, were the most natural things In the world to do.

Paul felt she was a queen whose actions must be left unquestioned.

Presently they came to a small village, and here she would land and lunch. And from somewhere behind the cabin Dmitry appeared, and was sent on ahead, so that when they walked into the little hotel a simple repast was waiting for them.

B5

THREE WEEKS

By this time Paul was absolutely enthralled. Never in his whole life had he spent such a morning. His imagination was expanded. He saw new vistas. His brain almost whirled. Was it he—Paul Verdayne—who was seated opposite this divine woman, drinking in her voice, and listening to her subtle curious thoughts?

And what were the commonplace, ordinary things which had hitherto occupied his mind.^ How had he ever wasted a moment on them ?

It was his first awakening.

When it came to the end—^this delightful repast—he called the waiter, and wanted to pay the bill; small enough in all conscience. But a new look appeared round the lady's mouth— imperious, with an instantaneous flash in her eyes—a pure, steel-grey they were to-day.

"Leave it to Dmitry," she said quickly. "I never occupy myself with money. They displease me, these details—and why spoil my day ?"

But Paul was an Englishman, and resented any woman's paying for his food. His mouth changed, too, and looked obstinate.

"I say, you know—" he began.

Then she turned upon him.

^ 54'

THREE WEEKS

"Understand at once," she said fiaugHtlly. "Either you leave me un jar red by your English conventionalities, or you pay these miserable francs and go back to Lucerne alone!"

Paul shrugged his shoulders. He viras angry, but could not insist further.

When they got outside, her voice grew caressing again as she led the way to a path up among the young beeches.

"Paul—foolish one!" she said. "Do you not think I understand and know you—and your quaint English ways? But imagine how silly it i:s. I am quite aware that you have ample money to provide me with a feast of Midas—all of gold —if necessary, and you shall some day, if you really wish. But to stop over paltry sums of francs, to destroy the thread of our conversation and thoughts—to make it all banal and everyday! That is what I won't have. Dmitry is there for nothing else but to eviter for me these details. It is my holiday, my pleasure-day, my time of joy. I felt young, Paul. You would not make one little shadow for me—would you, amif

No voice that he had ever dreamt of possessed so many tones in it as hers—even one of

ss

pathos, as she lingered over the word ^'shadow." All his annoyance melted. He only felt he would change the very mainspring of his life if necessary to give her pleasure and joy.

*'0f course I would not make a shadow,— surely you know that," he said, moved. "Only; you see a man generally pays for a woman'^ food."

"When she belongs to him—but I don't belong to you, baby Paul. You, for the day, belong to me—and are my guest!'*

"Very well, then, we won't talk about it," he said, resigned by the caress in her words. To belong to her! That was something, if but for one day.

"Only it must never come up again, this question," she insisted. "Should we spend more hours on this lake, or other lakes—or mountains, or rivers, or towns—let us speak never of money, or paying. If you only knew of how I hate it! the cruel yellow gold! I have heaps of it— heaps of it! and for it human beings have always paid so great a price. Just this once in life let it bring happiness and peace."

He wondered at the concentrated feeling she

expressed. What could the price be? And what was her history ?"

"So it is over, our little breeze,'* she said gently, after a pause. "And you will tease me no more, Paul?'*

"I would never tease you!" he exclaimed tenderly. And, if he had dared, he would have taken her hand.

"You English are so wonderful! Full of your prejudices," she said in a contemplative way. "Bulldog tenacity of purpose, whether you are right or wrong. Things are a custom, and they must be done, or it is not 'playing the game,' " and she imitated a set English voice, her beautiful mouth pursed up, until Paul had to use violent restraint with himself to keep from kissing it. "A wonderful people—mostly gentlemen and generally honest, but of a common sense that is disastrous to sentiment or romance. If you were not so polished, and lazy and strong—and beautiful to look at, one would not consider you much beyond the German."

"Not consider us beyond a beastly German!" exclaimed Paul indignantly.

And the lady laughed like a child.

"Oh! you darling Paul!" she said. "You dear, insular, arrogant Englishman! You have no equal in the world!"

Paul was offended.

"If you had said an Austrian now—^but a German—" he growled sulkily.

"The Austrians are charming," allowed the lady, "but they err the other way; they have not enough common sense, they are only great gentlemen. Also, they are naturally awake, whereas you English are naturally asleep, and you yourself are the Sleeping Beauty, Paul."

They had climbed up the path now some two hundred feet, and all around them were stripling beeches of an unnaturally exquisite green, as fresh and pure and light almost as leaves of the forced lily of the valley.

The whole world throbbed with youth and freshness, and here and there, wide of the path, by a mossy stone, a gentian raised its azure head, "small essences of sky," the lady called them.

"Let us sit down on this piece of rock," Paul said. "I want to hear why I am the Sleeping Beauty. It is so long since I read the story.

But wasn't it about a girl, not a man—and didn't she get wakened up by a—^kiss ?"

"She did!" said the lady, leaning back against a tree behind her; "but then it was just her faculties which were asleep, not her soul. Could a kiss wake a soul ?"

"I think so," Paul whispered. He was seated on a part of the rock which jutted out a little lower than her resting-place, and he was so close as to be almost touching her. He could look up under the brim of that tantalising hat, which so often hid her from his view as they walked. He was quivering with excitement at this moment, the result of the thought of a kiss—and his blue eyes blazed with desire as they devoured her face.

"Yes—it is so," said the lady, a low note in her voice. "Because Huldebrand gave Undine a soul with a kiss."

"Tell me about it," implored Paul. "I am so igruDrant. Who was Huldebrand, and what did he do?"

So she began in a dreamy voice, and you who have read De la Motte Fouque's dry version of this exquisite legend would hardly have recog-

nised the poetry and pathos and tender sentiment she wove round those two, and the varied moods of Undine, and the passion of her knight. And when she came to the evening of their wedding, when the young priest had placed their hands together, and Hstened to their vows—when Undine had found her soul at last, in Huldebrand's arms ■—her voice faltered, and she stopped and looked down.

"And then?'* said Paul, and his breath came rather fast. "And then ?"

"He was a man, you see, Paul; so when he had won her love, he did not value it—he threw it away."

"Oh, no! I don't believe it!" Paul exclaimed vehemently. "It was just this brute Huldebrand. But you don't know men—to think they do not value what they win—^you don't know them, indeed!"

She looked down straight into his face, as he gazed up at her, and to his intense surprise he could have sworn her eyes were green now! as green as emeralds. And they held him and fascinated him and paralysed him, like those of a snake.

"i do not know men ?" she said softly. "You think not, Paul?"

But Paul could hardly speak, he buried his face in her lap, like a child, and kept it there, kissing her gloved hands. His straw hat, with its Zin-gari ribbon, lay on the grass beside him, and a tiny shaft of sunlight glanced through the trees, gilding the crisp waves of his brushed-back hair into dark burnished gold.

The lady moved one hand from his impassioned caress, and touched the curl with her finger-tips. She smiled with the tenderness a mother might have done.

*There—there!" she said. "Not yet." Then she drew her hand away from him and leant back, half closing her eyes.

Paul sat up and stared around. Each moment of the day was providing new emotions for him. Surely this was what Columbus must have felt, nearing the new world. He pulled himself together. She was not angry then at his outburst, and his caress—though something in her face warned him not to err again.

"Tell me the rest," he said pleadingljr, "\Vhy

did he not value Undine's love, and what made the fool throw it away?"

"Because he possessed it, you see," said the lady. "That was reason enough, surely."

Then she told him of the ceasing of Undine's wayward moods after she had received her soul —of her docility—of her tenderness—of Hulde-brand's certainty of her love. Then of his inevitable weariness. And at last of the Court, and the meeting again with Hildegarde, and of all the sorrow that followed, until the end, when the fountains burst their stoppings and rushed upwards, v/reathing themselves into the figure of Undine, to take her Love to death with her kiss.

"Oh! he was wise!" Paul said. "He chose to die with her kiss. He knew at last then—^what he had thrown away."

"That one learns often, Paul, when it has grown—too late! Come, let us live in the sunshine. Live v/hile we may."

And the lady rose, and giving him her hand, she almost ran into the bright light of day, where even no tender shadows fell.

CHAPTER V/

THEIR return journey was one of quiet. The lady talked little, she leant back and looked away across the blue lake, often apparently unconscious of his presence. This troubled Paul. Had he wearied her? What should he do? He was growing aware of the fact that she was not a bit like his mother, or Isabella, or any of the other women whom he knew—people whose moods he had never even speculated about—if they had any—which he doubted.

Why wouldn't she speak? Had she forgotten him? He felt chilled and saddened.

At last, as they neared a small bay where another tempting little chalet-hotel mirrored itself in the clear water, he spoke. A note in his voice —his charming young voice—^as of a child in distress,

*'Are- are you cross with me?"

Then she came back from her other world. "Cross with you? FooHsh one! No, I am dreaming. And I forgot that you could nOt know yet, or understand. English Paul! who would have me make conversation and chatter commonplaces or he feels a gene! See, I will take you where I have been into this infinite sky and air"—she let her hand fall on his arm and thrilled him—"look up at Pilatus. Do you see his head so snowy, and all the delicate shadows upon him, and his look of mystery? And those (dark pines—and the great chasms, and the wild anger the giants were in when they hurled these huge rocks about? I have been with them, and you and I seem such little people, Paul. We cannot throw great rocks about—we are only two small ants in this grand world."

PauFs face was puzzled, he did not believe in giants. His mind was not accustomed yet to these flights of speech, he felt stupid and irritated with himself, and in some way humiliated. The lady leant over him, her face playfully tender.

"Great blue eyes!" she said. "So pretty, so

pretty! What matter whether they can see or no?" And she touched his lids with her slender fingers.

Paul quivered in his chair.

"You know!" he gasped. "You make me mad —I— But won't you teach me to see? No one wants to be blind! Teach me to see with your eyes, lady—my lady."

"Yes, I will teach you !'* she said. "Teach you a number of things. Together we will put on the hat of darkness and go down into Hades. We shall taste the apples of the Hesperides— we will rob Mercure of his sandals—and Gyges of his ring. And one day, Paul—when together we have fathomed the meaning of it all—what will happen then, enfant?"

Her last word, "enfant" was a caress, and Paul was too bewildered with joy to answer her for a moment.

"What will happen?" he said at last "I shall just love you—^that's all!"

Then he remembered Isabella Waring, and suddenly covered his face with his hands.

They stopped for tea at the quaint chalet-hotel, and after it they wandered to pick gentians. The

lady was sweet and sympathetic and gay; she ceased startling him with wild fancies; indeed, she spoke of simple everyday things, and got him to tell her of his home and Oxford, and his horses and his dogs. And when they arrived at the subject of Pike, her sympathy drew Paul nearer io her than ever. Of course she would love Pike if she only knew him! Who could help loving a dog like Pike ? And his master waxed eloquent. Then, when he looked away, the lady's weird chameleon eyes melted upon him in that strange tenderness which might have been a mother's watching the gambols of her babe.

The shadows were quite deep when at last they decided to return to Lucerne—a small bunch of heaven's own blue flower the only trophy of the day.

Paul had never enjoyed himself so much in his twenty-three years of life. And what would the evening bring? Surely more joy. This parting at the landing could not be good-night!

But as the launch glided nearer and nearer his heart fell, and at last he could bear the uncertainty no longer.

"And for dinner?" he said. "Won't you dine

with me, my Princess ? Let me be your host, as you have been mine all to-day."

But a stiffness seemed to fall upon her suddenly —she appeared to have become a stranger again almost.

*'Thank you, no. I cannot dine," she said. "I must write letters—and go to sleep."

Paul felt an ice-hand clutching his heart. Plis face became so blank as to almost pale before her eyes.

She leant forward, and smiled. "Will you be lonely, Paul ? Then at ten o'clock you must come under the ivy and wish me good-night."

And this was all he could gain from her. She landed hi.m to walk back to the hotel at the same place from which they had embarked, and the launch struck out again into the lake.

He walked fast, just to be near enough to see her step ashore on to the hotel wharf, but he could not arrive in time, and her grey figure disappearing up the terrace steps was all his hungry eyes were vouchsafed.

The weariness of dinner ? What did it matter what the food was? What did it matter that a new family of quite nice English people had ar-

rived, and sat near? A fresh young girl and a youth, and a father and mother. People who would certainly play billiards and probably bridge. What did anything matter in the world ? Time must be got through, simply got through until ten o'clock—that was all.

At half-past nine he strode out and sat upon the bench. His thoughts went back in a constant review of the day. How she had looked, where they had sat, what she had said. Why her eyes seemed green in the wood and blue on the water. Why her voice had all those tones in it. Why she had been old and young, and wise and childish. Then he thought of the story of Undine and the lady's strange, snake's look when she had said: "I do not know men ?—^You think not, Paul ?"

His heart gave a great bound at the remembrance. He permitted himself no speculation as to where he was drifting. He just sat there thrilling in every limb and every sense and every quality of his brain.

As the clocks chimed the hour something told him she was there above him, although he heard no sound.

Not a soul was in sight in this quiet comer.

He bounded on to the bench to be nearer—if she should come. If she were there hiding in the shadows. This was maddening—^unbearable. He would climb the balustrade to see. Then out of the blackest gloom came a laugh of silver. A soft laugh that was almost a caress. And suddenly she crept close and leant down over the ivy.

"Paul," she whispered. "I have come, you see, to wish you—good-night !"*

Paul stood up to his full height. He put out his arms to draw her to him, but she eluded him and darted aside.

He gave a great sigh of pain.

Slowly she came back and bent over and over of her own accord—so low that at last she was level with his face. And slowly her red lips melted into his young lips in a long, strange kiss.

Then, before Paul could grasp her, or murmur one pleading word, she was gone.

And again he found himself alone, intoxicated with emotion under the night sky studded with stars.

CHAPTER VI

RAIN, ram, rain? 'Tliat was not an agreeable sound to wake to when one had not had more than a few hours' sleep, and one's only hope of the day was to see one's lady again.

So Paul thought despairingly. What would happen? No lake, or mountain climb, was possible—but see her he must. After that kiss— that divine, enthralling, undreamed-of kiss. What did it mean? Did she love him? He loved her, that was certain. The poor feeble emotion he had experienced for Isabella was completely washed out and gone now.

He felt horribly ashamed of himself when he thought about it. His parents were perfectly right, of course; they had known best, and fortunately Isabella had not perhaps believed him, and was not a person of deep feeling anyway.

But the extreme discomfort of the thought of

her made him toss in his bed. What ought he to do ? Rush away from Lucerne ? To what good ? The die was cast, and in any case he was not bound to Isabella in any way. But at least he ought to write to her and tell her he had made a mistake. That was the only honest thing to do. A terrible duty, and he must brace himself up to accomplish it.

He breakfasted in his sitting-room, his thoughts scourging him the while, and afterwards, with a bulldog determination, he faced the writing-table and began.

He tore up at least three sheets to start with —no Greek lines of punishment in his boyhood had ever appeared such a task as this. He found himself scribbling profiles on the paper, chiselled profiles with inky hair—but no words would come.

"Dear Isabella," he wrote at last. No—"My dear Isabella," then he paused and bit the pen. "I feel I ought to tell you something has happened to me. I see my parents were right when—" "Oh! dash it all," he said to himself, "it's a beastly sneaking thing to do to put it like

THREE WEEKS

that," and he scratched the paragraph out and began again. "I have made a mistake in my feelings for you; I know now that they were those of a brother—" "O Lord, what am I to say next, it does sound bald, this!" The poor boy groaned and ran his hands through his curly hair, then seized the pen again, and continued— "as such I shall love you always, dear Isabella. Please forgive me if I have caused you any pain. It was all my fault, and I feel a beastly cad.— Your very unhappy Paul."

This was not a masterpiece! but it would have to do. So he copied it out on a fresh piece of paper. Then, when it was all finished and addressed he ran down and posted it himself in the hall, with some of the emotions Alexander may have experienced when he burnt his ships.

The clock struck eleven. At what time would he see the lady— his lady he called her now. Some instinct told him she did not wish the hotel people to be aware of their acquaintance. He felt it wiser not to send a note. He must wait and hope.

Rain or not, he was too English to stay indoors

THREE WEEKS

all day. So out he went and into the town. Tht quaint bridge pleased him; he tried to think how she would have told him to use his eyes. He must not be stupid, he said tO' himself, and already he began to perceive new meanings in things. Coming back, he chanced to stop and look in at the fur shop under the hotel. There were some nice skins there, and what caught his attention most was a really splendid tiger. A magnificent creature the beast must have been. The deepest, most perfectly marked, largest one he had ever seen. He stood for some time admiring it. An infinitely better specimen than his lady had over her couch. Should he buy it for her? Would she take it ? Would it please her to think he had remembered it might be what she would like?

He went into the shop. It was not even dear as tigers go, and his parents had given him ample money for any follies.

"Confound it, Henrietta! The boy must have his head!" Sir Charles Verdayne had said. "He's my son, you know, and you can't expect to cure him of one wench unless you provide him with shekels to buy another." Which crudely expressed wisdom had been followed, and Paul had

THREE WEEKS

no worries where his banking account was concerned.

He bought the tiger, and ordered it to be sent to his rooms immediately.

Then there was lunch to be thought of. She would not be there probably, but still he had a faint hope.

She was not there, nor were any preparations made for her; but when one is twenty-three and hungry, even if deeply in love, one must eat. The English people had the next table beyond the sacred one of the lady. The girl was pretty and young, and laughing. But what a doll! thought Paul. What a meaningless wax doll! Not worth —not worth a moment's glancing at.

And the pink and white fluffy girl was saying to herself: "There is Paul Verdayne again. I wish he remembered he had met me at the De Courcys', though we weren't introduced. I .must get Percy to scrape up a conversation with him. I wish mamma had not made me wear this green alpaca to-day." But Paul's blue eyes gazed through and beyond her, and saw her not. So all this prettiness was wasted.

And directly after lunch he returned to his sit-

ting-room. The tiger would probably have arrived, and he wanted to further examine it. Yes, it was there. He pulled it out and spread it over the floor. What a splendid creature—it reminded him in some way of her—his lady.

Then he went into his bedroom and fetched a pair of scissors, and proceeded to kneel on the floor and pare away the pinked-out black cloth which came beyond the skin. It looked banal, and he knew she would not like that.

Oh! he was awaking! this beautiful young Paul.

He had scarcely finished when there was a tap at the door, and Dmitry appeared with a note. The thin, remembered paper thrilled him, and he took it from the servant's hand.

"Paul—I am in the devil's mood to-day. About 5 o'clock come to me by the terrace steps."

That was all—there was no date or signature. But Paul's heart beat in his throat with joy,

"I want the skin to go to Madame," he said. "Have you any means of conveying it to her without the whole world seeing it go?"

The stately servant bowed. "If the Excellency would help him to fold it up," he said, "he would take it now to his own room, and from thence to the appartement niimero 3/"

It is not a very easy thing to fold up a huge tiger-skin into a brown paper parcel tied with string. But it was accomplished somehow and Dmitry disappeared noiselessly with it and an answer to the note:

"I will be there, sweet lady.

"Your own Paul."

And he was.

A bright fire burnt in the grate, and some palest orchid-mauve silk curtains were drawn in the lady's room when Paul entered from the terrace. And loveliest sight of all, in front of the fire, stretched at full length, was his tiger—and on him—also at full length—reclined the lady, garbed in some strange clinging garment of heavy purple crepe, its hem embroidered with gold, one white arm resting on the beast's head, her back supported by a pile of the velvet cushions, and a heap of rarely bound books at her

side, while between her red Hps was a rose not redder than they—^an almost scarlet rose. Paul had never seen one as red before.

The whole picture was barbaric. It might have been some painter's dream of the Favourite in a harem. It was not what one would expect to find in a sedate Swiss hotel.

She did not stir as he stepped in, dropping" the heavy curtains after him. She merely raised her eyes, and looked Paul through and through. Her whole expression was changed; it was wicked and dangerous and provocante. It seemed quite true, as she had said—she was evidently in the devil's mood.

Paul bounded forward, but she raised one hand to stop him.

"No! you must not come near me, Paul. I am not safe to-day. Not yet See, you must sit there and we will talk."

And she pointed to a great chair of Venetian workmanship and wonderful old velvet which was new to his view.

"I bought that chair in the town this morning at the curiosity shop on the top of Weggisstrasse, which long ago was the home of the Venetian

envoy here—^and you bought me the tiger, Paul. Ah! that was good. My beautiful tiger!" And she gave a movement like a snake, of joy to feel its fur under her, while she stretched out her hands and caressed the creature where the hair turned white and black at the side, and was deep and soft.

"Beautiful one? beautiful one!" she purred. "And I know all your feelings and your passions, and now I have got your skin—for the joy of my skin!" And she quivered again with the movements of a snake. '

It is not difficult to imagine that Paul felt far from calm during this scene—indeed he was obliged to hold on to his great chair to prevent himself from seizing her in his arms.

"I'm—Fm so glad you like him," he said in a choked voice. "I thought probably you would. And your own was not worthy of you. I found this by chance. And oh! good God! if you knew how you are making me feel—lying there wasting your caresses upon it!"

She tossed the scarlet rose over to him; it hit his mouth.

"I am not wasting them," she said, the innc^-

cence of a kitten in her strange eyes—^their colouf impossible to define to-day. "Indeed not, Paul! He was my lover in another life—perhaps—who knows ?"

"But I," said Paul, who was now quite mad, "want to be your lover in this!"

Then he gasped at his own boldness.

With a lightning movement she lay on her face, raised her elbows on the tiger's head, and supported her chin in her hands. Perfectly straight out her body was, the twisted purple drapery outlining her perfect shape, and flowing in graceful lines beyond—like a serpent's tail. The velvet pillows fell scattered at one side.

"Paul—what do you know of lovers—or love?" she said. "My baby Paul!"

"I know enough to know I know nothing yet which is worth knowing," he said confusedly. "But—^but—don't you understand, I want you to teach me—"

"You are so sweet, Paul! when you plead like that. I am taking in every bit of you. In your way as perfect as this tiger. But we must talk '—oh! such a great, great deal—first.'*

A rage of passion was racing through Paul, his incoherent thoughts were that he did not want to talk—only to kiss her—to devour her—^to strangle her with love if necessary.

He bit the rose.

"You see, Paul, love is a purely physical emo* tion," she continued. *'We could speak an immense amount about souls, and S3^mpathy, and understanding, and devotion. All beautiful things in their way, and possible to be enjoyed at a distance from one another. All the things which make passion noble—^but without love— which is passion—these things dwindle and become duties presently, when the hysterical exaltation cools. Love is tangible —it means to be close —close—to be clasped—to be touching—to be One!"

Her voice was low—so concentrated as to be startling in contrast to the drip of the rain outside, and her eyes—half closed and gleaming— burnt into his brain. It seemed as if strange flames of green darted from, their pupils.

*'But that is what I want!" Paul said, unsteadily.

"Without counting the cost? Tears and—

cold steel—and blood!" she whispered "Wait a while, beautiful Paul!"

He started back chilled for a second, and in that second she changed her position, pulling the cushions around her, nesthng into them and drawing herself cosily up like a child playing on a mat in front of the fire, while with a face of perfect innocence she looked up as she drew one of her great books nearer, and said in a dreamy; voice:

"Now we will read fairy-tales, Paul."

But Paul was too moved to speak. These rapid changes were too much for him, greatly advanced though he had become in these short days since he had known her. He leant back in his chair, every nerve in his body quivering, his young fresh face almost pale.

"Paul," she cooed plaintively, "to-morrow I shall be reasonable again, perhaps, and human, but to-day I am capricious and wayward, and mustn't be teased. I want to read about Cupid and Psyche from this wonderful 'Golden Ass' of Apuleius—^just a simple tale for a wet day—and you and—me!"

"Read then!" said Paul, resigned.

And she commenced in Latin, in a chanting, tender voice. Paul had forgotten most of the Latin he knew, but he remembered enough to be aware that this must be as easy as EngHsh to her as it flowed along in a rich rhythmic sound.

It soothed him. He seemed to be dreaming of flowery lands and running streams. After a while she looked up again, and then with one of her sudden movements like a graceful cat, she was beside him leaning from the back of his chair.

"Paul!" she whispered right in his ear, "am I being wicked for you to-day? I cannot help it. The devil is in me—and now I must sing."

"Sing then!" said Paul, maddened with again arising emotion.

She seized a guitar that lay near, and began in a soft voice in some language he knew not—a cadence of melody he had never heard, but one whose notes made strange quivers all up his spine. An exquisite pleasure of sound that was almost pain. And when he felt he could bear no more, she flung the instrument aside, and leant over his chair again—caressing his curls with her dainty

d>2

fingers, and purring unknown strange words in his ear.

Paul was young and unlearned in many things. He was completely enthralled and under her dominion—but he was naturally no weakling of body or mind. And this was more than he could stand.

"You mustn't be teased. My God! it is you who are maddening me!" he cried, his voice hoarse with emotion. "Do you think I am a statue, or a table, or chair—or inanimate like that tiger there? I am not, I tell you!" and he seized her in his arms, raining kisses upon her which, whatever they lacked in subtlety, made up for in their passion and strength. "Some day some man will kill you, I suppose, but I shall be your lover—first!"

The lady gasped. She looked up at him in bewildered surprise, as a child might do who sets a light to a whole box of matches in play. What a naughty, naughty toy to burn so quickly for such a little strike!

But Paul's young, strong arms held her close, she could not struggle or move. Then she. laughed a laugh of pure glad joy.

THREE WEEKS

"Beautiful, savage Paul," she whispered. "Do you love me? Tell me that?"

"Love you!" he said. "Good God! !Love you! Madly, and you knov: it, darling Queen."

"Then," said the lady in a voice in which all the caresses of the world seemed melted, "then, sweet Paul, I shall teach you many things, and among them I shall teach you how—to—Live.""

****

And outside the black storm made the darkness fall early. And inside the half-burnt logs tumbled together, causing a cloud of golden sparks, and then the flames leapt up again and crackled in the grate.

CHAPTER VII

AT dinner that night the lady came in after Paul was seated. She was all in black velvet, stately and dignified and fine. She passed his chair and took her seat, not the faintest sign of recognition on her face. And although he was prepared for this, for some reason his heart sank for a moment. Her demeanour was the same as on the first night he had seen her, hardly raising her eyes, eating little of the most exquisite food, and appearing totally unconscious of her neighbours or their ways. i She caused a flutter of excitement at the English table, the only other party, except two old men in a corner, who had dined so late, and they were half-way through their repast before she began hers. Paul was annoyed to see how they stared—stared at his lady. But what joy it was

THREE WEEKS

to sit there and realise that she was his—his very own! And only four nights ago he had been a rude stranger, too, criticising her every movement, and drinking too much port v/ith annoyance over it all. And now his whole life was changed. He saw with new eyes, and heard with new ears, even his casual observation was altered and sharpened, so that he noticed the texture of the cloth and the quality of the glass, and the shape of the room and its decoration.

And how insupportably commonplace the good English family seemed! That bread-and-butter miss with her pink cheeks and fluffy hair, without a hat! Wom.en's hair should be black and grow in heavy waves. He was certain of that now. How like them to come into a foreign restaurant hatless, just because they were English and must impose their customs! He sat and mused on it all, as he looked at his velvet-clad Queen. A sense of complete joy and satisfaction stealing over him, his wild excitement and emotion calmed for the time.

The delightful sensation of sharing a secret with her—a love-secret known only to themselves. Think, if these Philistines guessed at it

THREH WEEKS

even? their faces. And at this thought Paul almost laughed aloud.

With passionate interest he absorbed every little detail about his lady. How exactly she knew what suited her. How refined and grande dame and quiet it all was, and what an air of breeding and command she had in the poise of her little Greek head.

What did it matter what age she was, or of what nation? What did anything matter since she was his? And at that thought his heart began to beat again and cause him to speculate as to his evening.

W^ould she let him come back to the terrace room after dinner, or must he get through the time as best he could ? When he had left her, half dazed with joy and languor, no arrangements had been made—no definite plans settled. But of course she could not mean him not to wish her good-night—not now. For one second before she left the room their eves met, she raised a red rose, which she had taken from the silver vase, casually to her lips, and then passed out, but Paul knew she had meant the kiss for him, and his .whole being was uplifted.

THREE WEEKS

It was still pouring with rain. No possible excuse to smoke on the terrace. It might be wiser to stay in the hall. Surely Dmitry would come with some message before very long, if he was patient and waited her pleasure. But ten o'clock struck and there was no sign. Only the English youth, Percy Trevellian, had got into conversation with him, and was proposing billiards to pass the time.

Paul loved billiards—^but not to-night. Heavens ! what an idea! Go off to the billiard-room— now—^to-night!

He said he had a headache, and answered rather shortly in fact, and then, to escape further importunity, went up to his sitting-room, there to await the turn of events, leaving poor little Mabel Trevellian gazing after him with longing eyes.

"Did you see at dinner how he stared at that foreign person, mamma?" she said. "Men are such fools! Clarkson told me, as she fastened my dress to-night, she'd heard she was some Grand Duchess, or Queen, travelling incognito for her health. Very plain and odd-looking, didn't you think so, mamma? And quite old!"

"No, dear. Most distinguished. Not a girl,

THREE WEEKS

of course, but quite the appearance of a Princess," said Mabel's mother, who had seen the world.

Paul meanwhile paced his room—an anxious excitement was now his portion. Surely, surely she could not mean him not to see her—not to say one little good-night. What should he do? What possible plan invent ? As eleven chimed he could bear it no longer. Rain or no, he must go out on the terrace!

"Those mad English!" the porter said to himself, as he watched Paul's tall figure disappear in the dripping night.

And there till after twelve he paced the path under the trees. But no light showed; the terrace gate was locked. It vv^as chilly and wet and miserable, and at last he crept back utterly depressed, to bed. But not to sleep. Even his youth and health were not proof against the mad emotions of the day. He tossed and turned, a thousand questions singing in his brain. Was it really he who had been chosen b\'7d^ this divine woman for her lover? And if so, why was he alone now instead of holding her in his arms? What did it all mean? Who was she? Where would it end? But here he refused to think

THREE WEEKS

further. He was living at all events—living as he had never dreamed v^as possible.

And yet, poor Paul, he was only on the rim of all that he was soon to know of life.

At last he fell asleep, one sentence ringing in his ears—"Tears and—cold steel—and blood!" But if he was young, lie was a gallant gentleman, and Fear had no place in his dreams.

CHAPTER VIII

NEXT day they went to the Biirgenstock to stay. It was all arranged with consummate simplicity. Paul was to start for a climb, he told his valet, and for a week they would leave Lucerne. Mme. Zalenska was not very well, it appeared, and consented to try, at the suggestion of the amiable manager—inspired by Dmitry—a few days in higher air. There would not be a soul in their hotel on top of the Biirgenstock probably, and she could have complete rest.

They did not arrive together, Paul was the first. He had not seen her. Dmitry had given him his final instructions, and he awaited her coming with passionate impatience.

He had written to her, on awaking, a coherent torrent of love, marvellously unlike the letter which had gone to poor Isabella only a few days

before. In this to his lady he had said he could not bear it now, the uncertainty of seeing her, and had suggested the Biirgenstock crudely, without any of the clever details which afterwards made it possible.

He—Paul Verdayne, not quite twenty-three years old, and English—to suggest without a backward thought or a qualm that a lady whom he had known five days should come and live with him and be his love! None of his friends accustomed to his bashful habits would have believed it. Only his father perhaps might have smiled.

As for the Lady Henrietta, she would have fainted on the spot. But fortune favoured him —they did not know.

No excitement of the wildest day's hunting had ever made his pulses bound like this! Dmitry had arranged everything. Paul was a young English secretary to Madame, who had much writing to do. And in any case it is not the affair of respectable foreign hotels to pry into their clients' relationship when a large suite has been engaged.

Paul's valet, the son of an old retainer of the

family, was an honest fellow, and devoted to his master—but Sir Charles Verdayne had decided to make things doubly sure.

'Tompson," he had said, the morning before they left, "however Mr. Verdayne may amuse himself while you are abroad, your eyes and mouth are shut, remember. No d—d gossip back to the servants here, or in hotels, or houses —and, above all, no details must ever reach her Ladyship. If he gets into any thundering mess let me know—but mum's the word, d'y understand, Tompson?"

"I do. Sir Charles," said Tompson, stolidly.

And he did, as events proved.

The rooms on the Biirgenstock looked so simple, so unlike the sitting-room at Lucerne! Just fresh and clean and primitive. Paul wandered through them, and in the one allotted to himself he came upon Anna—Madame's maid, whom Dmitry had pointed out to him—putting sheets as fine as gossamer on his bed; with the softest down pillows. How dear of his lady to think thus of him!—her secretary.

The tiger—his tiger—had arrived in the sitting-room, and some simple cushions of silk;

sweet-peas and spring flowers decorated the vases —there were no tuberoses, or anything hot-house, or forced.

The sun blazed in at the windo^^^s, the green trees all washed and fresh from uie rain gladdened his eye, and down below, a sapphire lake reflected the snow-capped mountains. What a setting for a love-dream. No wonder Paul trod on air!

The only possible crumpled rose-leaves were some sentences in the lady's reply to his impassioned letter of the morning:

"Yes, I will come, Paul—^but only on one condition, that you never ask me questions as to who I am, or where I am going. You must promise me to take life as a summer holiday—an episode —and if fate gives us this great joy, you must not try to fetter me, now or at any future time, or control my movements. You must give me your word of honour for this—^you will never seek to discover who or what was your loved one—^you must never try to follow me. Yes, I will come for now—^when I have your assurance—but I will go when I will go—in silence."

And Paul had given his word. He felt he could not look ahead. He must just live in this gorgeous joy, and trust to chance. So he awaited her, thrilHng in all his being.

About tea time she drove up in a carriage—she and Dmitry having come the long way round.

And was it not right that her secretary should meet and assist her out, and conduct her to her apartments ?

How beautiful she looked, all in palest grey, and somehow the things had a younger shape. Her skirt was short, and he could see her small and slender feet, while a straw hat and veil adorned her black hair. Everything was simple, and as it should be for a mountain top and unsophisticated surroundings.

Tea was laid out on the balcony, fragrant Russian tea, and when Dmitry had lit the silver kettle lamp he retired and left them alone in peace.

"Darling!" said Paul, as he folded her in his arms—"darling!—darling!"

And when she could speak the lady cooed back to him:

"So sv/eet a word is that, my Paul. Sweeter in English than in any other language. And you

are glad I have come, and we shall live a little and be quite happy here in our pretty nest, all fresh and not a bit too grand—is it not so? Oh! what joys there are in life; and oh! how foolish just to miss them."

"Indeed, yes/' said Paul.

Then they played with the tea, and she showed him how he was to drink it with lemon. She was sweet as a girl, and said no vague, startling things; it was as if she were a young bride, and Paul were complete master and lord! Wild happiness rushed through him.. How had he ever endured the time before he had met her?

When they had finished they went out. She must walk, she said, and Paul, being English, must want exercise! Oh! she knew the English and their exercise! And of course she must think of everything that would be for the pleasure of her lover Paul.

And he? You old worn people of the world, who perhaps are reading, think what all this was to Paul—his young strong life vibrating to passionate joys, his imagination kindled, his very being uplifted and thrilled with happiness! His charming soul expanded, he found himself saying

gracious tender phrases to her. Every moment he was growing more passionately in love, and in each new mood she seemed the more divine. Not one trace of her waywardness of the day before remained. Her eyes, as they glanced at him from under her hat, were bashful and sweet, no look of the devil to provoke a saint. She talked gently.

He must talce her to the place where she had peeped at him through the trees. And—

"Oh! Paul!" she said. "If you had known that day, how you tempted me, looking up at me, your whole soul in your ^yes! I had to run, run, run!" ^

"And now I have caught you, darling mine," said Paul. "But you were wrong. I had no soul—it is you who are giving me one now."

They sat on the bench where he had sat. She was getting joy out of the colour of the moss, the tints of the beeches, every little shade and shape of nature, and letting Paul see with her eyes.

And all the while she was nestling near him like a tender ring-dove to her mate. Paul's heart

THREE WEEKS

swelled with exultation. He felt good, as if he could be kind to every one, as if his temper were a thing to be ashamed of, and all his faults, as if for ever he must be her own true knight and defender, and show her he was worthy of this great gift and joy. And ah! how could he put into words his tender worshipping love ?

So the afternoon faded into evening, and the young crescent moon began to show in the sky— a slender moon of silver, only born the night before.

"See, this is our moon," said the lady, "and as she waxes, so will our love wax—^but now she is young and fresh and fair, like it. Come, ray Paul. Let us go to our house; soon we shall dine, and I want to be beautiful for you."

So they went in to their little hotel.

She was all in white when Paul found her in their inner salon, where they were to dine alone, waited on only by Dmitry. Her splendid hair was bound with a fillet of gold, and fell in two long strands, twisted with gold, nearly to her knees. Her garment was soft and clinging, and unlike ;^ny garment he had ever seen. They sat

THREE WEEKS

on a sofa together, the table in front of them, and they ate slowly and whispered much— and before Paul could taste his wine, she kissed his glass and sipped from it and made him do the same with hers. The food was of the simplest, and the only things exotic were the great red strawberries at the end.

Dmitry had left them, placing the coffee on the table as he went, and a bottle of the rare golden wine.

Then this strange lady grew more tender still. She must lie in Paul's arms, and he must feed her with strawberries. And the thought came to him that her mouth looked as red as they.

To say he was intoxicated with pleasure and love is to put it as it was. It seemed as if he had arrived at a zenith, and yet he knew there would be more to come. At last she raised herself and poured out the yellow wine—into one glass.

"My Paul," she said, "this is our wedding night, and this is our wedding wine. Taste from this our glass and say if it is good."

And to the day of his death, if ever Paul should taste that wine again, a mad current of passion-

THREE WEEKS

ate remembrance will come to him—and still more passionate regret.

Oh! the divine joy of that night! They sat upon the balcony presently, and Elaine in her worshipping thoughts of Lancelot—Marguerite wooed by Faust—the youngest girl bride—could not have been more sweet or tender or submissive than this wayv^^ard Tiger Queen.

"Paul," she said, "out of the whole world tonight there are only you and I who matter, sweetheart. Is it not so ? And is not that your English word for lover and loved—'sweetheart' ?"

And Paul, who had never even heard it used except in a kind of joke, now knew it was what he had always admired. Yes, indeed, it was "sweetheart"—and she was his!

"Remember, Paul," she whispered when, passion maddening him, he clasped her violently in his arms—"remember—whatever happens— whatever comes—for now, to-night, there is no other reason in all of this but just—I love you--I love you, Paul!"

"My Queen, my Queen!" said Paul, his voice hoarse in his throat.

And the wind played in softest zephyrs, and

the stars blazed in the sky, mirroring themselves in the blue lake below.

Such was their wedding night.

Oh! glorious youth! and still more glorious love!

CHAPTER IX

WHO can tell the joy of their awakening-? The transcendent pleasure to Paul to be allowed to play with his lady's hair, all unbound for him to do with as he willed? The glory to realise she was his— his own—in his arms ? And then to be tenderly masterful and give himself lordly airs of possession. She was almost silent, only the history of the whole world of passion seemed written in her eyes—slumbrous, inscrutable, their heavy lashes making shadows on her soft^ smooth cheeks.

The ring-dove was gone, a thing of mystery lay there instead—unresisting, motionless, white. Now and then Paul looked at her half in fear. Was she real? Was it some dream, and would he wake in his room at Verdayne Place among the sporting prints and solid Chippendale furniture to hear Tompson saying, "Eight o'clock, sir, and a fine day" ?

102

/

Oh, no, no, she was real! He raised himself, and bent down to touch her tenderly with his forefinger. Yes, all this fascination was indeed his, living and breathing and warm, and he was her lover and lord. Ah!

The same coloured orchid-mauve silk curtains as at Lucerne were drawn over the open windows, so the sun in high heaven seemed only as dawn in the room, filtering though the jalousies outside. But what was time? Time counts as one lives, and Paul was living now.

It was twelve o'clock before they were ready for their dainty breakfast, laid out under the balcony awning.

And the lady talked tenderly and occupied herself with the fancies of her lord, as a new bride should.

But all the time the mystery stayed in her eyes. And the thought came to Paul that were he to live with her for a hundred years, he would never be sure of their real meaning.

"What shall we do with our day, my Paul?" she said presently. "See, you shall choose. Shall we climb to the highest point on this mountain and look at our kingdom of trees and lake below ?

,103

Or shall we rest in the launch and glide over the blue water, and dream sweet dreams? Or shall we drive in the carriage far inland to a quaint farmhouse I know, where we shall see people living in simple happiness with their cows and their sheep? Decide, sweetheart—decide!"

"Whatever you would wish, my Queen," ffaid Paul.

Then the lady frowned, and summer lightnings flashed from her eyes.

*'0f course, w^hat I shall wish! But I have told you to choose, feeble Paul! There is nothing so irritates me as these English answers. Should I have asked you to select our day had I decided myself? I would have commanded Dmitry to make the arrangements, that is all. But no! to-day I am thy obedient one. I ask my Love to choose for me. To-morrow I may want my own will; to-day I desire only thine, beloved," and she leant forward and looked into his eyes.

"The mountain top, then!" said Paul, "because there we can sit, and I can gaze at you, and learn more of life, close to your lips. I might not touch you in the launch, and you might look at others at the farm—^and it seems as if I could not

THREE WEEKS

bear one glance or word turned from myself today!"

*'You have chosen well. Mylyi inoi."

The strange words pleased him; he must know their meaning, and learn to pronounce them himself. And all this between their dainty dishes took time, so it was an hour later before they started for their walk.

Up, up those winding paths among the firs and larches—^up and up to the top. They dawdled slowly until they reached their goal. There, aloof from the beaten track, safe from the prying eyes of some chance stranger, they sat down, their backs against a giant rock, and all the glory of their lake and tree-tops to gaze at down below.

Paul had carried her cloak, and now they spread it out, covering their couch of moss and lichen. A soft languor was over them both. Passion was asleep for the while. But what exquisite bliss to sit thus, undisturbed in their eyrie —^lie and she alone in all the world.

Her words came back to him: *'Love means to be clasped, to be close, to be touching, to be One!" Yes, they were One.

THREE WEEKS

Then she began to talk softly, to open yet more windows in his soul to joy and sunshine. Her mind seemed so vast, each hour gave him fresh surprises in the perception of her infinite knowledge, while she charmed his fancy by her delicate modes of expression and un-English perfect pronunciation, no single word slurred over.

"Paul," she said presently, "how small seem the puny conventions of the world, do they not, beloved ? Small as those little boats floating like scattered flower-leaves on the great lake down there. They were invented first to fill the place of the zest which fighting and holding one's own by the strength of one's arm originally gave to man. Now, he has only laws to combat, instead of a fiercer fellow creature—a dull exchange forsooth ! Here are you and I—mated and wedded and perfectly happy—and yet by these foolish laws we are sinning, and you would be more nobly employed yawning with some bony English miss for your wife—and I by the side of a mad, drunken husband. All because the law made us swear a vow to keep for ever stationary an emotion! Emotion which we can no more control than the trees can which way the wind will blow

THREE WEEKS

their branches! To love! Oh! yes, they call it that at the altar—^joined together by God!' As likely as not two human creatures who hate each other, and are standing there swearing those impossibilities for some political purpose and advantage of their family. They desecrate the word love. Love is for us, Paul, who came together because our beings cried, *This is my mate!* I should say nothing of it—oh no! if it had no pretence—marriage. If it were frankly a contract —

Yes, I give you my body and my dowry. *Yes, you give me your name and your state.' It is of the coarse, horrible things one must pass through in life—but to call the Great Spirit's blessing upon it, as an exaltation! To stand there and talk of love! Ah—that is what must miake God angry, and I feel for Him."

Paul noticed that she spoke as if she had no realisation of the lives of lesser persons who might possibly wed because they were "mated" as well—not for political reasons or ambition of family. Her keen senses divined his thought.

"Yes, beloved, you would say—?"

"Only that supposing you were not married to any one else, we should be sv/earing the truth

if we swore before God that we loved. I would make any vows to you from my soul, in perfect honesty, for ever and ever, my darling Queen."

His blue eyes, brimming with devotion and conviction of the truth of his thought, gazed up at her. And into her strange orbs there came that same look of tenderness that once before had made them as a mother's watching the gambols of her babe.

"There, there," she said. "You would swear them and hug your chains of roses—^but because they were chains they would turn heavy as lead. Make no vows, sweetheart! Fate will force you to break them if you do, and then the gods are angry and misfortune follows. Swear none, and that fickle one will keep you passionate, in hopes always to lure you into her pitfalls—^to vow and to break—pain and regret. Live, live, Paul, and love, and swear nothing at all."

Paul was troubled. "But, but," he said, "don't you believe I shall love you for ever?"

The lady leant back against the rock and narrowed her eyes.

"That will depend upon me, my Paul," she said. *'Jhe duration of love in a being always

depends upon the loved one. I create an emotion in you, as you create one in me. You do not create it in yourself. It is because something in my personality causes an answering glow in yours that you love me. Were you to cease to do so, it would be because I was no longer able to call forth that answer in you. It would not be your fault any more than when you cease to please me it will be mine. That is where people are unjust."

"But surely," said Paul, "it is only the fickle who can change?"

"It is according to one's nature; if one is bom a. steadfast gentleman, one is more likely to continue than if one is a farceur —prince or no—but it depends upon the object of one's love— whether he or she can hold one or not. One would not blame a needle if it fell from a magnet, the attraction of the magnet being in some w^ay removed, either by a stronger at the needle's side, or by some deadening of the drawing quality in the magnet itself—^and so it is in love. Do you follow me, Paul?"

"Yes," said Paul gloomily. "I must try to please you, or you will throw me away."

"You see/* she continued, "the ignorant mafe vows, and being weakhngs—for the most part—• vanity and fate easily remove their inclination from the loved one; it may not be his fault any more than a broken leg keeping him from walking would be his fault, beyond the fact that it was his leg; but we have to suffer for our own things—so there it is. We will say the weakling's inclination wants to make him break his vows; so he does, either in the letter or spirit—or both! And then he feels degraded and cheap and low, as all must do who break their sacred word given of their own free will when inclina-lion prompted them to. So how much better to make no vow; then at least when the cord of attraction snaps, we can go free, still defying the lightning in our untarnished pride."

"Oh! darling, do not speak of it," cried Paul, "the cord of attraction between us can never snap. I worship, I adore you—you are just my life, my darling one, my Queen!"

"Sweet Paul!" she whispered, "oh! so good, so good is love, keep me loving you, my beautiful one—keep my desire long to be your Queen."

And after this they melted into one another's

THREE WEEKS

arms, and cooed and kissed, and were foolish and incoherent, as lovers always are and have been from the beginning- of old time. More concentrated—more absorbed—than the sternest Eastern sage—absorbed in each other.

The spirit of two natures vibrating as One.

CHAPTER X

THAT evening it was so warm and peaceful they dined at the wide-open balcony windows. They could see far away over the terrace and down to the lake, with the distant lights towards Lucerne. The moon, still slender and fine, was drawing to her setting, and a few cloudlets floated over the sky, obscuring the stars here and there.

The lady was quiet and tender, her eyes melting upon Paul, and something of her ring-dove mood was upon her again. Not once, since they had been on the Bijrgenstock, had she shown any of the tigerish waywardness that he had had glimpses of at first. It seemed as if her moods, like her chameleon eyes, took colour from her surroundings, and there all was primitive simplicity and nature and peace.

Paul himself was in a state of ecstasy. He hardly knew whether he trod on air or no. No siren of old Greek fable had ever lured mortal

THREE iVEEKS

more under her spell than this strange foreign woman thing—Queen or Princess or what you will. Nothing else in the world was of any consequence to him—and it was all the more remarkable because subjection was in no way part of his nature. Paul was a masterful youth, and ruled things to his will in his own home.

The lady talked of him—of his tastes—of his pleasures. There was not an incident in his life, or of his family, that she had not fathomed by now. All about Isabella even^—poor Isabella! And she told him how she sympathised with the girl, and how badly he had behaved.

"Another proof, my Paul, of what I said today—no one must make vows about love."

But Paul, in his heart, believed her not. He would worship her for ever, he knew.

"Yes," she said, answering his thoughts. "You think so, beloved, and it may be so because you do not know from moment to moment how I shall be—if I shall stay here in your arms, or fly far away beyond your reach. You love me because I give you the stimulus of uncertainty, and so keep bright your passion, but once you were sure, I should become a duty, as all women be-

THREE WEEKS

come, and then my Paul would yawn and grow to see I was no longer young, and that the expected is always an ennui when it comes!"

"Never, never!" said Paul, with fervour.

Presently their conversation drifted to other things, and Paul told her how he longed to see the world and its people and its ways. She had been almost everywhere, it seemed, and with her talent of word-painting, she took him with her on the magic carpet of her vivid description to east and west and north and south.

Oh! their entr'actes between the incoherence of just lovers' love were not banal or dull. And never she forgot her tender ways of insinuated caresses—small exquisite touches of sentiment and grace. The note ever of One—^that they were fused and melted together into one body and soul.

Through all her talk that night Paul caught glimpses of the life of a great lady, surrounded with state and cares, and now and then there was a savage echo which made him think of things barbaric, and wonder more than ever from whence she had come.

It was quite late before the chill of night airs

9rove them into their salon, and here sHe made him some Russian tea, and then lay in his arms, and purred love-words to him, and nestled close like a child who wants petting to cure it of some imaginary hurt. Only, in her tenderest caresses he seemed at last to feel something of danger. A slumbering look of passion far under the calm exterior, but ready to break forth at any moment from its studied control.

It thrilled and maddened him.

"Beloved, beloved!" he cried, "let us waste no more precious moments. I want you—I want you—my sweet!"

At the first glow of dawn, he awoke, a strange sensation, almost of strangling and suffocation, upon him. There, bending over, framed in a mist of blue-black waves, he saw his lady's face. Its milky whiteness lit by her strange eyes— green as cats' they seemed, and blazing with the fiercest passion of love—while twisted round his throat he felt a great strand of her splendid hair. The wildest thrill as yet his life had known then came to Paul; he clasped her in his arms with a frenzy of mad, passionate joy.

CHAPTER XI

THE next day was Sunday, and even through the silk blinds they could hear the rain drip in monotonous fashion. Of what use to wake? Sleep is blissful and calm when the loved one is near.

Thus it was late when Paul at last opened his eyes. He found himself alone, and heard his lady's voice singing softly from the sitting-room beyond, and through the open door he could perceive her stretched on the tiger, already dressed, reclining among the silk pillows, her guitar held in her hands.

"Hasten, hasten, lazy one. Thy breakfast awaits thee," she called, and Paul bounded up without further delay.

This day was to be a day of books, she said, and she read poetry to him, and made him read to her—but she would not permit him to sit too near her, or caress her—and often she was restless

and moved about with the undulating grace of a cat. She would peep from the windows, and frown at the scene. The lake was hidden by mist, t'ae skies cried, all nature was weeping and gloon^y.

And at last she hung the books aside, and crept up to Paul, who was huddled on the sofa, feeling rather morose from her decree that he must not touch or kiss her,

"Weeping skies, I hate you!'* she said. Then she called Dmitry in a sharp voice, and when he appeared from the passage where he always awaited her pleasure, she spoke to him in Russian, or some language Paul knew not, a fierce gleam in her eyes. Dmitry abased himself almost to the floor, and departing quickly, returned with sticks and lit a blazing pine-log fire in the open grate. Then he threw some powder into it, and with stealthy haste drew all the orchid-silk curtains, and departed from the room. A strange divine scent presently rose in the air, and over Paul seemed to steal a spell. The lady crept still nearer, and then with infinite sweetness, all her docility of the first hours of their union returned, she melted in his arms.

"Paul—I am so wayward to-day, forgive me," she said in a childish, lisping voice. "See, I will make you forget the rain and damp. Fly with me to Egypt where the sun always shines."

And Paul, like a sulky, hungry b^by, who had been debarred, and now received its expected sweetmeat, clasped her and kissed her for a few minutes before he would let her speak.

"See, we are getting near Cairo," she said, her eyes half closed, while she settled herself among the cushions, and drew Paul down to^ her until his head rested on her breast, and her arms held him like a mother with a child.

Her voice was a dream-voice as she whispered on. "Do you not love those minarets and towers against the opal sky, and the rose-pink granite hills beyond? And look, Paul, at this peep of the Nile—those are the water-buffaloes—^those strange beasts—you see they are pulling that ridiculous water-drawer—just the same as in Pharaoh's time. Ah! I smell the scent of the East. Look at the straight blue figures, the lines so pleasing and long. The dignity, the peace, the forever in it all. . . . Now we are there. See the brilliant crowd all moving with little

haste, and listen to the strange noise. Look at the faces of the camels, disdainful and calm, and that of an old devil-man with tangled hair. . . .

"Come—come from this; I want the desert and the Sphinx!

'Ah! it is bright day again, and we have all the green world between us and the great vast brown tract of sand. And those are the Pyramids clear-cut against the turquoise sky, and soon we shall be there, only 3^ou must observe this green around us first, my Paul—the green of no other country in all the world—^pure emerald—■ nature's supreme concentrated effort of green for miles and miles. No, I do not want to live in that small village in a brown mud hut, shared with another w^ife to that gaunt blue linen-clad man; I would kill them all and be free. I want to go on, beloved—on to the desert for you and me alone, with its wonderful passion, and wonderful peace. . . .'

Her voice became still more dreamy; there was a cadence in it now as if some soul within were forcing her to chant it all, with almost the lilt of blank verse.

"Oh! the strange drug of the glorious East, flooding your senses with beauty and life. 'Tis the spell of the Sphinx, and now we are there, close in her presence. Look, the sun has

wV7L« • • •

*TIush! hush! beloved! we are alone, the camels and guides afar off—we are alone, sweetheart, and we go on together, you and I and the moon. See, she is rising all silver and pure, and blue is the sky, and scented the night. Look, there is the Sphinx! Do yon see the strange mystery of her smile and the glamour of her eyes ? She is a goddess, and she knows men's souls, and their foolish unavailing passion and pain—never content with the Is which they have, always regretting the Was which has passed, and building false hopes on the phantom May he. But you and I, my lover, my sweet, have fathomed the riddle which is hid in the smile of our goddess, our

Sphinx—^we have guessed it, and now are as high gods too. For we know it means to live in the present, and quaff life in its full. Sweetheart, beloved— ^joy and life in its full " ,

£20

Her voice grew faint and far away, like the echo of some exquisite song, and the lids closed over Paul's blue eyes, and he slept.

The light of all the love in the world seemed to flood the lady's face. She bent over and kissed him, and smoothed his cheek with her velvet cheek, she moved so that his curly lashes might touch her bare neck, and at last she slipped from under him, and laid his head gently down upon the pillows.

Then a madness of tender caressing seized her. She purred as a tiger might have done, while she undulated like a snake. She touched him with her finger-tips, she kissed his throat, his wrists, the palms of his hands, his eyelids, his hair. Strange, subtle kisses, unlike the kisses o£ women. And often, between her purrings, she murmured love-words in some strange fierce language of her own, brushing his ears and his eyes with her lips the while.

And through it all Paul slept on, the Eastern perfume in the air still drugging his sense.

It was quite dark when he awoke again, and beside him—seated on the floor, all propped with pillows, his lady reclined her head against his

shoulder. And as he looked dov/n at her In the firelight's flickering- gleam, he saw that her wonderful eyes were wet with great glittering tears.

**My soul, my soul!" he said tenderly, his heart wrung with emotion. "What is it, sweetheart— why have you these tears? Oh! what have I done—darling, my own?"

"I am weary," she said, and fell to weeping softly, and refused to be comforted.

Paul's distress was intense—^what could have happened? What terrible thing had he done? What sorrow had fallen upon his beloved while he selfishly slept? But all she would say was that she was weary, while she clung to him in a storm of passion, as if some one threatened to take her out of his arms. Then she left him abruptly and went off to dress.

But later, at dinner, it seemed as if a new and more radiant light than ever glowed on her face. She was gay and caressing, telling him m.erry tales of Paris and its plays. It was as if she meant to efface all suggestion of sorrow or pain —and gradually the impression wore off in Paul's mind, and ere it came to their sipping the golden v/ine, all was brightness and peace.

"See," she said, looking from the window Just before they retired to rest, "the sky has stopped crying, and there are our stars, sweetheart, come out to wish us good-night. Ah! for us to-morrow once more will be a glorious day."

"My Queen," said Paul; "rain or fine, all days are glorious to me, so long as I have you to clasp in my arms. You are my sun, moon and stars—always, for ever."

She laughed a laugh, the silver echo of satisfaction and joy.

"Sweet Paul," she lisped mischievously, "so good you have been, so gentle with my moods. You must have some reward. Listen, beloved I while I tell it to you."

But what she said is written in his heart I

CHAPTER Xir

HIS lady was so intensely soignee —^that is what pleased Paul. He had never thought about such things, or noticed them much in other women, but she was a revelation.

No Roman Empress w^ith her bath of asses' milk could have had a more wonderful toilet than she. And ever she was illusive, and he never quite got to the end of her mystery. Always there was a veil, when he least expected it, and so these hours for the most part were passed at the boiling-point of excitement and bliss. The experiences of another man's whole lifetime Paul was going through in the space of days.

It was the Monday following the wet Sunday when an incident happened which soon came back to him, and gave him food for reflection.

They Vv^ould spend the day in the launch, she decided, going whither they wished, stopping here

to pick gentians, going there under the shadow of trees—landing where and when they desired —even sleeping at Fliielen if the fancy took them to. Anna was sent on with their things in case this contingency occurred. And earth, water and sky seemed smiling them a welcome.

Just before they started, Dmitry, after the gentlest tap, noiselessly entered Paul's room. Paul was selecting somxe cigars from a box, and looked up in surprise as the stately servant cautiously closed the door.

*'Yes, Dmitry, what is it?" he said half impatiently.

Dmitry advanced, and now Paul saw that he carried something in his hand. He bowed low with his usual courtly respect. Then he stammered a little as he began to speak.

The substance of his sentence, Paul gathered, was that the Excellency would not be inconveniencing himself too much, he hoped, if he would consent to carry this pistol. A very good pistol, he assured him, which would take but little room.

Paul's surprise deepened. Carry a pistol in peaceful Switzerland! It seemed too absurd.

"What on earth for, my friend?" he said.

But Dmitry would give no decided answer, only that it was wiser, when away from one's home and out with a lady, never to go unarmed. Real anxiety peeped from his cautious grey eyes.

Did Paul know how to shoot ? And would he be pardoned for asking the Excellency such a question?—^but in England, he heard, they dealt little with revolvers—and this was a point to be assured of.

Yes, Paul knew how to shoot! The idea made him laugh. But now he came to think of it, he had not had great practice with a revolver, and might not do so well as with a gun or rifle. But the whole thing seemed so absurd, he did not think it of much consequence.

"Of course I'll take it to please you, Dmitry," he said, "though I wish you would tell me why."

However, Dmitry escaped from the room without further words, his finger upon his lips.

The lady was looking more exquisitely white than usual; she wore soft pale mauve, and appeared in Paul's eyes a thing of joy.

When they were seated on the launch in their chairs, she let him hold her hand, but she did not

talk much at first; only now he understood Her silences, and did not worry over them—so great a teacher is love to quicken the perception of man.

He sat there, and gazed at her, and tried to realise that it was really he who was experiencing all this happiness. This wonderful, wonderful woman—and he was her lover.

At last something in her expression of sadness caught his watchful eye, and an ache came into his mind to know where hers had gone.

"Darling," he said tenderly, "mayn't I come there, too?"

She turned towards him—a shadow was in her eyes.

"No, Paul," she said. "Not there. It is a land of rocks and precipices—not for lovers."

"But if you can go—where is the danger for me, my Queen? Or, if there is danger, then it is my place to stand by your side."

"Paul, my sweet Paul," she whispered, while her eyes filled with mist, "I was thinking how fair the world could be, perhaps, if fate allowed one to meet one's mate while there was yet time. Surely two souls together, like you and I, might climb to Paradise doing deeds of greatness by the

way. But so much of life is like a rushing torrent tearing along making a course for itself, without power to choose through what country it will pass, until it meets the ocean and is swallowed up and lost. If one could only see—only know in time—could he change the course? Alas! who can tell ?*

Her voice was sad, and as ever it wrung Paul's heart.

"Aly darling one," he said, "don't think of those odd things. Only remember that I am here beside you, and that I love you, love you so—"

"My Paul!" she murmured, and she smiled a strange, sweet smile, "do you know, I find you like a rare violin which hitherto has been used by ordinary musicians to play their popular airs upon, but which is now highly strung and being touched by the bow of an artist who loves it. And oh! the exquisite sounds which are coming, and will yet come forth to enchant the ear, and satisfy the sense. All the capacity is there, Paul, in you, beautiful one—only I must bring it out with my bow of love! And what a progress you have made already—a great, great progress. Think, only a few days ago you had never noticed

the colours of this lake, or even these great mountains, they said nothing to you at all except as places to take your exercise upon. Life, for you, was just eating and sleeping and strengthening your muscles." And she laughed softly.

*'! know I was a Goth," said Paul. "I can hardly realise it myself, the change that has happened to me. Everything now seems full of joy."

"Your very phrases are altered, Paul, and will alter more yet, while our moon waxes and our love grows."

"Can it grow? Can I possibly love you more intensely than I do now—surely nol" he exclaimed passionately. "And yet—" - ^ ^ •

"And yet?"

"Ah! yes, I know it. Yes, it can grow until it is my life—my very life."

"Yes, Paul," she said, "your life"—and her strange eyes narrowed again, the Sphinx's inscrutable look of mystery in their chameleon depths.

Then her mood altered, she became gay and laug;hing, and her wit sparkled like dry cham-

pagne, while the white launch glided through the blue waters with never a swirl of foam.

"Paul," she said presently, "to-morrow we will go up the Rigi to the Kaltbad, and look from the little kiosk over the world, and over the Bernese Oberland. It gives me an emotion to stand so high and see so vast a view—^but to-day we will play on the water and among the trees."

He had no desires except to do what she would do, so they landed for lunch at one of the many little inviting hotels which border the lake in sheltered bays. All through the meal she entertained him with subtle flattery, drawing him out, and making him shine until he made flint for her steel. And when they came to the end she said with sudden, tender sweetness:

"Paul—it is my caprice—^you may pay the bill I to-day—^just for to-day—because—Ah! you must guess, my Paul! the reason why V*

And she ran out into the sunlight, her cheeks bright pink.

But Paul knew it was because now she belonged to him. His heart swelled with joy—^and who so proud as he ?

She had gone alone up a mountain path when

THREE WEEKS

he came out to join her, and stood there laughing at him provokingly from above. He bounded up and caught her, and would walk hand in hand, and made her feel that he was master and lord through the strength of his splendid, vigorous youth. He pretended to scold her if she stirred from him, and made her stand or walk and obey him, and gave himself the airs of a husband and prince.

And the lady laughed in pure ecstatic joy. "Oh! I love you, my Paul—like this, like this! Beautiful one! Just a splendid primitive savage beneath the grace, as a man should be. When I feel how strong you are my heart melts with bliss!"

And Paul, to show her it was true, seized her in his arms, and ran with her, placing her on a high rock, where he made her pay him with kisses and tell him she loved him before he would lift her down.

And it was his lady's caprice, as she said, that this state of things should last all day. But by night time, when they got to Fliielen, the infinite mastery of her mind, and the uncertainty of his

THREE WEEKS

hold over her, made her his Queen again, and Paul once more her worshipping slave.

Now, although his master was quite oblivious of posts, Tompson was not, and that Monday he took occasion to go into Lucerne, whence he returned with a pile of letters, which Paul found on again reaching the Biirgenstock, after staying the night at Fliielen in a little hotel.

That had been an experience! His lady quite childish in her glee at the smallness and simplicity of everything.

"Our picnic," she called it to Paul—only it was a wonderfully recherche picnic, as Anna of course had brought everything which was required by heart of sybarite for the passing of a night.

Ah! they had been happy. The Queen had been exquisitely gracious to her slave, and entranced him more deeply than ever. And here at the Biirgenstock, when he got into his room, his letters stared him in the face.

"Damned officiousness!" he said to himself, thinking of Tompson.

He did not want to be reminded of any exist-

THREE WEEKS

ence other than the dream of heaven he was now enjoying".

Oh! they were all very real and material, these epistles—quite of earth! One was from his mother. He was enjoying Lucerne, she hoped, and she was longing for his return. She expected he also was craving for his home and horses and dogs. All were well. They—she and his father—^were moving up to the town house in Berkeley Square the following week until the end of June, and great preparations were already in contemplation for his twenty-third birthday in July at Verdayne Place. There was no mention of Isabella except a paragraph at the end. Miss Waring was visiting friends at Blackheath, he was informed. Ah, so far away it all seemed! But it brought him back from heaven. The next was his father's writing. Laconic, but to the point. This parent hoped he was not wasting his time—d—d short in life! and that he was cured of his folly for the parson's girl, and found other eyes shone bright. If he wanted more money he was to say so.

Several were from his friends, banal and everyday. And one was from Tremlett, his own

groom, and this was full of Moonlighter and— Pike! That gave him just a moment's feeling— Pike! Tremlett had *'made so bold" as to have some snapshots done by a friend, and he ventured to send one to his master. The "very pictur' " of the dog, he said, and it was true. Ah! this touched him, this little photograph of Pike.

"Dear little chap," he said to himself as he looked. "My dear little chap."

And then an instantaneous desire to show it to his lady came over him, and he went back to the sitting-room in haste.

There she was—^the post had come for her too, it seemed, and she looked up with an expression of concentrated fierceness from a missive she was reading as he entered the room. Her marvellous self-control banished all but love from her eyes after they had rested on him for an instant, but his senses—so fine now—had remarked the first glance, just as his eye had seen the heavy royal crown on the paper as she hastily folded it and threw it carelessly aside.

"Darling!" he said. "Oh! look! here is a picture of Pike!"

And if it had been the most important document concerning the fate of nations the lady could not have examined it with more enthralled interest and attention than she did this snapshot photograph of a rough terrier dog.

"What a sweet fellow!" she said. "Look at his eye! so intelligent; look at that patte! See, even he is asking one to love him—and I do—I do—"

"DarHng!" said Paul in ecstasy, "oh, if we only had him here, wouldn't that be good !'*

And he never knew why his lady suddenly threw her arms round his neck, and kissed him with passionate tenderness and love, her eyes soft as a dove's.

"Oh, my Paul," she said, a break in her wonderful voice, whose tones said many things, "my young, darling, English Paul!"

Presently they would drive to see that quaint farm she wanted to show him. The day was very warm, and to rest in the comfortable carriage would be nice. Paul thought so, too. So after a late lunch they started. And once or twice on the drive through the most peaceful and beautiful scenery, a flash of the same fierceness

came into the lady's eyes, gazing away over distance as when she had read her letter, and it made Paul wonder and long to ask her why. He never allowed himself to speculate in coherent thought words even as to who she was, or her abode in life. He had given his word, and was an Englishman and would keep it, that was all. But in his subconsciousness there dwelt the conviction that she must be some Queen or Princess of a country south in Europe—half barbaric, half advanced. That she was unhappy and hated it all, he more than divined. It was a proof of the strength of his character that he did not let the terrible thought of inevitable parting mar the bliss of the tangible now. He had promised her to live while the srn of their union shone, and he had the force to keep his word.

But oh! he wished he could drive all care from her path, and that this glorious life should go on for ever.

When they got to the farm in the soft late afternoon light, the most gracious mood came over his lady. It was just a Swiss farmhouse of many storeys, the lower one for the cows and other animals, and the rest for the family and in-

THREE WEEKS

dustries. All was clean and in order, with that wonderful outside neatness which makes Swiss chalets look like painted toy houses popped down on the greensward without yard or byre. And these people were well-to-do, and it was the best of its kind.

The Bauerin, a buxom mother of many little ones, was nursing another not four weeks old, a fat, prosperous infant in its quaint Swiss clothes. Her broad face beamed with pride as she welcomed the gracious lady. Old acquaintances they appeared, and they exchanged greetings. Foreign languages were not Paul's strong point, and he caught not a word of meaning in the German patois the good woman talked. But his lady was voluble, and seemed to know each flaxen-haired child by name, though it was the infant which longest arrested her attention. She held it in her arms. And Paul had never seen her look so young or so beautiful.

The good woman left them alone while she prepared some coffee for them in the adjoining kitchen, followed by her troop of kinder. Only the little one still lay in the lady's arms. She spoke not a word—she sang; to it a cradle-song,

and the thought came to Paul that she seemed as an angel, and this must be an echo of his own early heaven before his life had descended to earth.

A strange peace came over him as he sat there watching her, his thoughts vague and dreamy of some beautiful sweet tenderness—he knew not what.

Ere the woman returned with the coffee the lady looked up from her crooning and met his eyes—all her soul was aglow in hers—while she whispered as he bent over to meet her lips:

"Yes, some day, my sweetheart—^yes."

And that magic current of sympathy which was between them made Paul know what she meant. And the gladness of the gods fell upon him and exalted him, and his blue eyes swam with tears.

Ah! that was a thought, if that could ever be!

All the way back in the carriage he could only kiss her. Their emotion seemed too deep for words.

And this night was the most divine of any they had spent on the Biirgenstock. But there was in it an essence abgilt which only the angels could write.

CHAPTER XIII

DO you know the Belvedere at the Rigi Kaltbad, looking over the comer to a vast world below, on a fair day in May, when the air is clear as crystal and the lake ultramarine? When the Bernese Oberland undulates away in unbroken snow, its pure whiteness like cold marble, the shadows grey-blue?

Have you seen the tints of the beeches, of the pines, of the firs, clinging like some cloak of life to the hoary-headed mountains, a reminder that spring is eternal, and youth must have its day, however grey beards and white heads may frown ?

Ah—it is good!

And so is the air up there. Hungry and strong and—^young.

Paul and his lady stood and looked down in rapt silence. It was giving her, as she said, an

emotion, but of what sort he was not sure. They were all alone. No living soul was anywhere in view.

She had been in a mood all day when she seldom raised her eyes. It reminded him of the first time he had seen her, and wonder grew again in his mind. All the last night her soul had seemed melted into his in a fusion of tenderness and trust, exalted with the exquisite thought of the wish which was between them. And he had felt at last he had fathomed its inmost recess.

But to-day, as he gazed down at her white-rose paleness, the heavy lashes making their violet shadow on her cheek—her red mouth mutinous and full—the conviction came back to him that there were breadths and depths and heights about which he had no conception even. And an ice hand clutched his heart. Of what strange thing was she thinking? leaning over the parapet there, her delicate nostrils quivering now and then.

"Paul," she said at last, **did you ever want to kill any one? Did you ever long to have them there at your mercy, to choke their life out and throw them to hell ?"

"Good God, no!" said Paul aghast.

THREE WEEKS

Then at last she looked up at him, and her eyes were black with hate. "Well, I do, Paul. I would like to kill one man on earth—a useless, vicious weakling, too feeble to deserve a fine death—a rotting carrion spoiHng God's world and encumbering my path! I would kill him if I could—and more than ever to-day.'*

'0h, my Queen, my Queen!" said Paul, distressed. "Don't say such things—^you, my own tender woman and love—'

"Yes, that is one side of me, and the best— but there is another, which he draws forth, and that is the worst. You of calm England do not know what it means—the true passion of hate."

"Can I do nothing for you, beloved?" Paul asked. Here was a phase which he had not yet seen.

"Ah!" she said, bitterly, and threw up her head. "No! his high place protects him. But for his life I would conquer all fate."

"Darling, darling—" said Paul, who knew not what to say.

"But, Paul, if a hair of your head should be hurt, I would kill him myself with these my own hands."

THREE WEEKS

Once Paul had seen two tigers fight in a travelling circus-van which came to Oxford, and now the memory of the scene returned to him when he looked at his lady's face. He had not known a human countenance could express such fierce, terrible rage. A quiver ran through him. Yes, this was no idle boast of an angry woman—he felt those slender hands would indeed be capable of dealing death to any one who robbed her of her mate.

But what passion was here! What force! He had somehow never even dreamt such feelings dwelt in women—or, indeed, in any human creatures out of sensational books. Yet, gazing there at her, he dimly understood that in himself, too, they could rise, were another to take her from him. Yes, he could kill in suchlike case.

They were silent for some moments, each vibrating with passionate thoughts; and then the lady leant over and laid her cheek against the sleeve of his coat.

"Heart of my heart," she said, "I frighten and ruffle you. The women of your country are sweet and soft, but they know not the passion I

THREE WEEKS

know, my Paul—^the fierceness and madness oV love—"

Paul clasped her in his arms.

"It makes me worship you more, my Queen," he said. Englishwomen would seem like wax dolls now beside you and your exquisite face— they will never again be anything but shadows in my life. It can only hold you, the one goddess and Queen."

Her eyes were suffused with a mist of tenderness, the passion was gone; her head was thrown back against his breast, when suddenly her hand inadvertently touched against the pocket where Dmitry's pistol lay. She started violently, and before he could divine her purpose she snatched the weapon out, and held it up to the light.

Her face went like death, and for a second she leant against the parapet as if she were going to faint.

"Paul," she gasped with white lips, "this is Dmitry's pistol. I know it well. How did you come by it?—tell me, beloved. If he gave it to you, then it means danger, Paul—danger—"

"My darling," said Paul, in his strong young pridcr *'fear nothing, I shall never leave you.

I

will protect you from any danger in the world, only depend upon me, sweetheart. Nothing can hurt you while I am here."

*'Do you think I care a sou for my life?" she said, while she stood straight up again with the majesty of a queen. **Do you think I feared for me—for myself? Oh I no, my own lover, never that! They can kill me when they choose, but they won't; it is you for whom I fear. Only your danger could make me cower, no other in the whole world."

Paul laughed with joy at her speech. "There is nothing to fear at all then, darling," he said. "I can take care of myself, you know. I am an Englishman."

And even in the tumult of her thoughts the lady found time to smile with tender amusement at the young insular arrogance of his last words. An Englishman, forsooth! Of course that meant a kind of god untouched by the failings of other nations. A great rush of pride in him came over her and gladdened her. He was indeed a splendid picture of youth and strength, as he stood there, the sunlight gilding his fair hair, and all the magnificent proportions of his figure thrown

into relief against the background of grey sione and sky, an insoiiciante smile on his h'ps, and all the light of love and self-confidence in his fine blue eyes.

She responded to the fire in them, and appeared to grow comforted and at peace. But all the way back through the wood to the Kaltbad Hotel she glanced furtively into the shadows, while she talked gaily as she held Paul's arm.

And he never asked her a question as to where she expected the danger to come from. No anxiety for his own safety troubled him one jot —indeed, an unwonted extra excitement flooded his veins, making him enjoy himself with an added zest.

Dmitry as usual awaited them at the hotel; his face was serene, but when Paul's back was turned for a moment while he lit a cigarette, the lady questioned her servant with whispered fierceness in the Russian tongue. Apparently his answer was satisfactory, for she looked relieved, and presently, seated on the terrace, they had a merry tea—the last they would have on mountain tops, for she broke it gently to Paul tliat on the morrow she must return to Lucerne. Paul felt as if

liis heart had stopped beating. Return to Lucerne ! O God! not to part—surely not to part— so soon!

"No, no," she said, the thought making her whiten too. "Oh no! my Paul, not that—^yet!"

Ah—^he could bear anything if it did not mean parting, and he used no arguments to dissuade her. She was his Queen and must surely know best. Only he listened eagerly for details of how matters could be arranged there. Alas! they could never be the same as this glorious time they had had.

"You must wait two days, sweetheart," she said, "before you follow me. Stay still in our nest if you will, but do not come on to Lucerne."

"I could not stand it," said Paul. "Oh I darling, don't kill me with aching for your presence two whole days! It is a lifetime! not to be endured—"

"Impatient one!" she laughed softly. "No— neither could I bear not to see you, sweetheart, but we must not be foolish. You must stay on in our rooms and each morning I will meet you somewhere in the launch. Dmitry knows every inch of the lake, and we can pass most of our days thus, happy at last—"

"But the nights!" said Paul, deep distress in his voice. "What on earth do you think I can do with the nights ?'*

"Spend them in sleep, my beloved one," the lady said, while she smiled a soft fine smile.

But to Paul this idea presented the poorest compensation—and in spite of his will to the contrary his thoughts flew ahead for an instant to the inevitable days and nights when— Ah! no, he could not face the picture. Life would be finished for him when that time came.

The thought of only a temporary parting on the morrow made them cling together for this, their last evening, with almost greater closeness and tenderness than usual. Paul could hardly bear his lady out of his sight, even while she dressed for dinner, when they got back to the Burgenstock, and twice he came to the door and asked plaintively how long she would be, until jA.nna took pity on him, and implored to be allowed to ask him to come in while she finished her mistress's hair. And that was a joy to Paul! He sat there by the dressing-table, and played

THREE WEEKS

with the things, opening the Hds of gold boxes, and sniffing bottles of scent with an air of right and possession which made his lady smile like a purring cat. Then he tried on her rings, but they would only go on to the second joint of his little finger, as he laughingly showed her—and finally he pushed Anna aside, and insisted upon putting the last touches himself to the glorious waves of black hair.

And all the while he teased the maid, and chaffed her in infamous French, to her great delight, while his lady looked at him, whole wells of tenderness deep in her eyes.

Paul had adorable ways when he chose. No wonder both mistress and maid should worship him.

The moon was growing larger, her slender contours more developed, and the stars seemed fainter and farther off. Nothing more exquisite could be dreamed of, thought Paul, than the view from their balcony windows, the light on the silver snows. And he would let no thought that it was the last night they would see it together mar the passionate joy of the hours still to be. His lady had never been more sweet; it was as

THREE WEEKS,

if this wayward Undine had at last found her soul, and lay conquered and unresisting in her lover's strong arms.

Thus in perfect peace and happiness they passed their last night on the Biirgenstock.

CHAPTER XIV

THE desolation which came over Paul when next day before lunch time he found himself alone on the terrace, looking down vainly trying to distinguish his lady^s launch as it glided over the blue waters, seemed unendurable. An intense depression filled his being. It was as if a limb had been torn from him; he felt helpless and incomplete, and his whole soul drawn to Lucerne.

The green trees and the exquisite day seemed to mock him. Alone, alone—with no prospect of seeing his Queen until the morrow, when at eleven he was to meet her at the landing-steps at the foot of the funiculaire.

But that was to-morrow, and how could he get through to-day?

After an early lunch he climbed to their rock at the summit, and sat there where they had sat together—alone with his thoughts.

THREE WEEKS

And what thoughts!

What was this marvellous thing which Had happened to him? A fortnight ago he was in

Paris, disgusted with everything around him, and fancying himself in love with Isabella Waring. Poor Isabella! How had such things ever been possible? Why, he was a schoolboy then—a child—an infant! and now he was a man, and knew what life meant in its greatest and best. That was part of the wonder of this lady, with all her intense sensuousness and absence of what European nations call morality; there was yet nothing low or degrading in her influence, its tendency was to exalt and elevate into broad views and logical reasonings. Nothing small would ever again appeal to Paul. His whole outlook was vaster and more full of wide thoughts.

And then among the other emotions in his breast came one of deep gratitude to her. For, apart from her love, had she not given him the royalest gift which mankind could receive—^an awakened soul ? Like her story of Undine it had truly been bom with that first long kiss.

Then his mind flew to their after-kisses, tKe immense divine bliss of these whole six days.

THREE WEEKS

Was it only six days since they had come there? Six days of Paradise. And surely fate would not part them now. Surely more hours of joy lay in store for them yet. The moon was seven days old—and his lady had said, "While she waxes our love will wax." Thus, even by that calculation, there was still time to live a little longer. \

Paul's will was strong. He sternly banished all speculations as to the future. He remembered her counsel of the riddle which lay hidden in the eyes of the Sphinx—to live in the present and quaff life in its full.

Pie was in a mood of such worship that he could have kissed the grey rock because she had leant against it. And to himself he made vows that, come what might, he would ever try to be worthy of her great spirit and teaching. Dmitry's pistol still lay in his pocket; he took it out and examined it—^all six chambers were loaded. A deadly small thing, with a finely engraved stock made in Paris. There was a date scratched. It was about a year old.

What danger could they possibly have dreaded for him?—^he almost laughed. He stayed up on

THREE WEEKS

the highest point until after the sun had set; somehow he dreaded going back to the rooms where' they had been so happy—going back alone! But this was weakness, and he must get over the feeling. After dinner he would spend the evening writing his letters home. But when this solitary meal was over, the moon tempted him out on to the terrace, and there he stayed obsessed with passionate thoughts until he crept in to his lonely couch.

He could not sleep. It had no memories there to comfort him. He got up, and went across the sitting-room to the room his lady had left so lately. Alas! it was all dismantled of her beautiful things. The bed unmade and piled with uncovered hotel pillows, and a large German eiderdown, on top of folded blankets, it all looked ghastly and sad and cold. And more depressed than ever he crept back to his own bed.

Next morning was grey—not raining, but dull grey clouds all over the sky. Not a tempting prospect to spend it in a launch on the lake. A wind, too, swept the w^ater into small rough wavelets. Would she come? The uncertainty was sJmost agony. He was waiting long before the

THREE WEEKS

time appointed, and walked up and down anxiously scanning the direction towards Lucerne.

. Yes, that was the launch making its way along, not a moment late. Oh! what joy thrilled his being! He glowed all over—in ten minutes or less he could clasp her hands.

But when the launch came in full view, he perceived no lady was there—only Dmitry's black form stood alone by the chairs.

Paul's heart sank like lead. He could hardly contain his anxiety until the servant stepped ashore and handed him a letter, and this was its contents:

"My beloved one —^I am not well to-day—a foolish chill. Nothing of consequence, only the cold wind of the lake I could not face. At one o'clock, when Lucerne is at lunch, come to me by the terrace gate. Come to me, I cannot live without you, Paul."

"What is it, Dmitry?" he said anxiously. "Madame is not ill, is she ? Tell me—"

"Not ill—oh no!" the servant said, only Paul must know Madame was of a delicacy at times

THREE WEEKS

in the cold weather, and had to be careful of herself. He added, too, that it would be wiser if Paul would lunch early before they started, because, as he explained, it was not for the people of the hotel to know he was there, and how else could he eat ?

All of which advice was followed, and at one o'clock they landed at Lucerne, and Paul walked quickly towards his goal, Dmitry in front to see that the way was clear. Yes—^there was no one about for the moment, and like ghosts they glided through the little terrace door, and Paul went into the room by the window, while Dmitry held the heavy curtains, and then disappeared.

It was empty—the fact struck a chill note, in spite of the great bowls of flowers and the exquisite scent. His tiger was there, and the velvet pillows of old. All was warm and luxurious, as befitting the shrine of his goddess and Queen. Only he was alone—alone with his thoughts.

An incredible excitement swept through him, his heart beat to suffocation in the longing for her to come. Was it possible—^was it true that soon she would be in his arms ? A whole world

THREE WEEKS

of privation and empty hours to make up for in their first kiss.

Then from behind the screen of the door to her room she came at last—a stately figure in long black draperies, her face startlingly white, and her head wrapped in a mist of black veil. But who can tell of the note of gladness and welcome she put into the two words, "My Paul!" ?

And who can tell of the passionate joy of their long, tender embrace, or of their talk of each one's impossible night? His lady, too, had not slept, it appeared. She had cried, she said, and fought with her pillow, and been so wicked to Anna that the good creature had wept. She had torn her fine night raiment, and bitten a handkerchief through! But now he had come, and her soul was at rest. What wonder, when all this was said in his ear with soft, broken sighs and kisses divine, that Paul should feel like a god in his pride!

Then he held her at arms'-length and looked at her face. Yes, it was very pale indeed, and the violet shadows lay under her black lashes. Had she suffered^ his darling;—was she ill ? But

56

I

THREE WEEKS

no, the fire in her strange eyes gave no look of ill-health.

"I was frightened, my own," he said, "in case you were really not well. I must pet and take care of you all the day. See, you must lie on the sofa among the cushions, and I will sit beside you and soothe you to rest." And he lifted her in his strong arms and carried her to the couch as if she had been a baby, and settled her there, every touch a caress.

His lady delighted in these exhibitions of his strength. He had grown to understand that he could always affect her when he pretended to dominate her by sheer brute force. She had explained it to him thus one day:

"You see, Paul, a man can always keep a woman loving him if he kiss her enough, and make her feel that there is no use struggling because he is too strong to resist. A woman will stand almost anything from a passionate lover. He may beat her and pain her soft flesh; he may shut her up and deprive her of all other friends-while the motive is raging love and interest in herself on his part, it only makes her love him the more. The reason why women become unfaith-

fill IS because the man grows casual, and having awakened a taste for passionate joys, he no longer gratifies them—so she yawns and turns elsewhere."

Well, there was no fear of her doing so if he could help it! He was more than willing to follow this receipt. Indeed, there was something about her so agitating and alluring that he knew in his heart all men would feel the same towards her in a more or less degree, and wild jealousy coursed through his veins at the thought.

"My Paul," she said, "do you know I have a plan in my head that we shall go to Venice ?"

"To Venice!" said Paul in delight. "To Venice!"

"Yes—I cannot endure any more of Lucerne, parted from you, with only the prospect of snatched meetings. It is not to be borne. We shall go to that home of strange joy, my lover, and there for a space at least we can live in peace."

Paul asked no better gift of fate. Venice he had always longed to see, and now to see it with her! Ah! the very thought was ecstasy to him, and made the blood bound in his veins.

"When, when, my darling?" he asked. "Tomorrow ? When ?"

"To-day is Friday," she said. *'One must give Dmitry time to make the arrangements and take a palace for us. Shall we say Sunday, Paul ? I shall go on Sunday, and you can follow the next day—so by Tuesday evening we shall be together again, not to part until—the end."

"The end?" said Paul, with sinking heart.

"Sweetheart," she whispered, while she drew his face down to hers, "think nothing evil. I said the end—but fate alone knows when that must be. Do not let us force her hand by speculating about it. Remember always to live while we may."

And Paul was more or less comforted, but in moments of silence all through the day he seemed to hear the echo of the words—^The End.

CHAPTER XV

IT was a beautiful apartment that Dmitry had found for them on the Grand Canal in Venice, in an old palace looking southwest. A convenient door In a side canal cloaked the exit and entry of its inhabitants from curious eyes— had there been any to indulge in curiosity; but in Venice there is a good deal of the feeling of live and let live, and the dolce far niente of the life is not conducive to an over-anxious interest in the doings of one's neighbours.

Money and intelligence can achieve a number of things in a short space of time, and Dmitry had had both at his command, so everything, Including a chef from Paris and a retinue of Italian servants, was ready when on the Tuesday evening Paul arrived at the station. i ;What a wonderland it seemed to him, Venice! A wonderland where was awaiting him his heart's

delight—^more passionately desired than ever after three days of total abstinence.

As after the Friday afternoon he had spent more or less in hiding- in the terrace-room, his lady had judged it wiser for him not to come at all to Lucerne, and on the Saturday had met him at a quiet part of the shore of the lake, beyond the landing-steps of the funiculaire, and for a few short hours they had cruised about on the blue waters—but her sweetest tenderness and ready wit had not been able entirely to eliminate the feeling of unrest which troubled them. And then there were the nights, the miserable evenings and nights of separation. On the Sunday she had departed to Venice, and after she had gone, Paul had returned for one day to Lucerne, leaving again on the Monday, apparently as unacquainted with Madame Zalenska as he had been the first night of his arrival.

He had not seen her since Saturday. Three whole days of anguishing longing. And now in half an hour at least she would be in his arms. The journey through the beautiful scenery froni Lucerne had been got through at night—all day from Milan a feverish excitement had dominated

him, and prevented his taking any interest in outward surroundings. A magnetic attraction seemed drawing him on—on—^to the centre of light and joy—his lady's presence.

Dmitry and an Italian servant awaited his arrival; not an instant's delay for luggage called a halt. Tompson and the Italian were left for that, and Paul departed with his trusty guide.

It was about seven o'clock, the opalescent lights were beginning to show in the sky, and their reflection in the water, as he stooped his tall head to enter the covered gondola. It was all too beautiful and wonderful to take in at once, and then he only wanted wings the sooner to arrive, not eyes to see the passing objects. Afterwards the strange soft cry of the gondoliers and the sights appealed to him; but on this first evening every throb of his being was centred upon the one moment when he should hold his beloved one to his heart.

He could hardly contain his impatience, and walk sedately beside Dmitry when they ascended the great stone staircase—he felt like bounding up three steps at a time. Dmitry had been respectfully silent. Madame was well—^that was

all he would say. He opened the great double door with a latch-key, and Paul found himself in t% vast hall almost unfurnished but for some tapestry on the walls, and a huge gilt marriage-chest, and a couple of chairs. It was ill lit, and there was something of decay and gloom in its aspect.

On they went, through other doors to a salon, vast and gloomy too, and then the glory and joy of heaven seemed to spring upon Paul's view when the shrine of the goddess was reached—a smaller room, whose windows faced the Grand Canal, now illuminated by the setting sun in all its splendour, coming in shafts from the balcony blinds. And among the quaintest and most old-world surroundings, mixed with her own wonderful personal notes of luxury, his lady rose from the tiger couch to meet him.

His lady! His Queen!

And, indeed, she seemed a queen when at last he held her at arms'-length to look at her. She was garbed all ready for dinner in a marvellous garment of shimmering purple, while round her shoulders a scarf of brilliant pale emerald gauze, all fringed with gold, fell in two long ends, and

on her neck and in her ears great emeralds gleamed—a pear-shaped one of unusual brilliancy fell at the parting of her waves of hair on to her white smooth forehead. But the colour of her eyes he could not be sure of—only they were two wells of love and passion gazing into his own.

All the simplicity of the Burgenstock surroundings was gone. The flowers were in the greatest profusion, rare and heavy-scented; the pillows of the couch were more splendid than ever; cloths of gold and silver and wonderful shades of orange and green velvet were among the purple ones he already knew. Priceless pieces of brocade interwoven with gold covered the screens and other couches; and, near enough to pick up when she wanted them, stood jewelled boxes of cigarettes and bonbons, and stands of perfume.

Her expression, too, was altered. A new mood shone there; and later, when Paul learnt the history of the wonderful women of cinquecento Venice, it seemed as if something of their exotic voluptuous spirit now lived in her.

This was a new queen to worship—and die for, if necessary. He dimly felt, even in these first

moments, that here he would drink still deeper of the mysteries of life and passionate love.

"Beztzenny-moi" she said, "my priceless one. At last I have you again to make me live. Ah I I must know it is really you, my Paul!"

They were sitting on the tiger by now, and she undulated round and all over him, feeling his coat, and his face, and his hair, as a blind person might, till at last it seemed as if she were twined about him like a serpent. And every now and then a narrow shaft of the glorious dying sunlight would strike the great emerald on her forehead, and give forth sparks of vivid green which appeared reflected again in her eyes. Paul's head swam, he felt intoxicated with bliss. \

"This Venice is for you and me, my Paul," sHe said. "The air is full of love and dreams; we have left the slender moon behind us in Switzerland; here she is nearing her full, and the summer is upon us with all her richness and completeness—^the spring of our love has passed." ;

Her voice fell into its rhythmical cadence, as if she were whispering a prophecy inspired by; some presence beyond.

"We will drink deep of the cup of delight, my^

lover, and bathe in the wine of the gods. We shall feast on the tongues of nightingales, and rest on couches of flowers. And thou shalt cede me thy soul, beloved, and I will give thee mine—" But the rest was lost in the meeting of their lips.

♦ ♦ ♦ -Ic 4: ^ ^

They dined on the open loggia, its curtains drawn, hiding them from the view of the palaces opposite, but not preventing the soft sounds of the singers in the gondolas moored to the poles beneath from reaching their ears. And above the music now and then would come the faint splash of water, and the **Stahi"—"Preme" of some moving gondolier.

The food was of the richest, beginning with strange fishes and quantities of hors d/oeuvres that Paul knew not, accompanied by vodka in several forms. And some of the plats she would just taste, and some send instantly away.

And all the while a little fountain of her own perfume played from a group of sportive cupids in silver, while the table in the centre was piled with red roses. Dmitry and two Italian foot-

men waited, and everything was done witfi tlie greatest state. A regal magnificence was in the lady's air and mien. She spoke of the splendours of Venice's past, and let Paul feel the atmosphere of that subtle time of passion and life. Of here a love-scene, and there a murder. Of wisdom and vice, and intoxicating emotion, all blended in a kaleidoscope of gorgeousness and colour.

And once again her vast Icnowledge came as a fresh wonder to Paul—^no smallest detail of history seemed wanting in her talk, so that he lived again in that old world and felt himself a Doge.

When they were alone at last, tasting the golden wine, she rose and drew him to the loggia balustrade. Dmitry had drawn back the curtains and extinguished the lights, and only the brilliant moon lit the scene; a splendid moon, two nights from the full. There she shone straight down upon them to welcome them to this City of Romance.

What loveliness met Paul's view! A loveliness in which art and nature blended in one satisfying whole.

"Darling," he said, "this is better than the
THREE WEEKS
Biirgenstock. Let us go out on the water and float about, too."

It was exceedingly warm these last days of May, and that night not a zephyr stirred a ripple. A cloak and scarf of black gauze soon hid the lady's splendour, and they descended the staircase hand in hand to the waiting open gondola.

It was a new experience of joy for Paul to recline there, and drift away down the stream, amidst the music and the coloured lanterns, and the wonderful, wonderful spell of the place.

The lady was silent for a while, and then she began to whisper passionate words of love. She had never before been thus carried away—and he must say them to her—as he held her hand— burning words, inflaming the imagination and exciting the sense. It seemed as if all the other nights of love were concentrated into this one in its perfect joy.

Who can tell of the wild exaltation which filled Paul? He was no longer just Paul Verdayne, the ordinary young Englishman; he was a god— and this was Olympus.

"Look, Paul r' she said at last. "Can you not
THREE WEEKS
see Desdemona peeping- from the balcony of her house there ? And to think she will have no happiness before her Moor will strangle her to-night! Death without joys. Ah! that is cruel. Some joys are wxll worth death, are they not, my lover, as you and I should know?"

"Worth death and eternity," said Paul. "For one such night as this with you a man would sell his soul."

It was not until they turned at the opening of the Guidecca to return to their palazzo that they both became aware of another gondola following them, always at the same distance behind—a gondola with two solitary figures in it huddled on the seats.

The lady gave a whispered order in Italian to her gondolier, who came to a sudden stop, thus forcing the other boat to come much nearer before it, too, arrested its course. There a moonbeam caught the faces of the men as they leant forward to see what had occurred. One of them was Dmitry, and the other a younger man of the pure Kalmuck type whom Paul had never seen.

"Vasili!" exclaimed the lady, in passionate surprise. "yasiH! and they have not told me!"
THREE WEEKS
She trembled all over, while her eyes blazed green flames of anger and excitement. "If it is unnecessary they shall feel the whip for this."

Her cloak had fallen aside a little, disclosing a shimmer of purple garment and flashing emeralds. She looked barbaric, her raven brows knit. It might have been Cleopatra commanding the instant death of an offending slave.

It made Paul's pulses bound, it seemed so of the picture and the night. All was a mad dream of exotic emotion, and this was just an extra note.

But who was Vasili ? And what did his presence portend? Something fateful at all events.

The lady did not speak further, only by the quiver of her nostrils and the gleam in her eyes he knew how deeply she was stirred.

Yes, one or the other would feel the whip, if they had been over-zealous in their duties!

It seemed out of sheer defiance of some fate that she decided to go on into the lagoon when they passed San Georgio. It was growing late, and Paul's thoughts had turned to greater joys. He longed to clasp her in his arms, to hold her, and prove her his own. But she sat there, her

THREE WEEKS

small head held high, and her eyes fearless and' proud—thus he did not dare to plead with her.

But presently, when she perceived the servants were no longer following, her mood changed, the sweetness of the serpent of old Nile fell upon her, and all of love that can be expressed in whispered words and tender hand-clasps, she lavished upon Paul, after ordering the gondolier to hasten back to the palazzo. It seemed as if she, too, could not contain her impatience to be again in her lover's arms.

"I will not question them to-night," she said when they arrived, and she saw Dmitry awaiting Her on the steps. "To-night we will live and love at least, my Paul. Live and love in passionate bliss r

But she could not repress the flash of her eyes which appeared to annihilate the old servant. He fell on his knees with the murmured words of supplication:

"O Imperatorskoye!" And Paul guessed it meant Imperial Highness, and a great wonder grew in his mind.

Their supper was laid in the loggia again, and under the windows the musicians still played and

THREE WEEKS

sang a gentle accompaniment to their sighs of

love.

• But later still Paul learnt what fiercest passion meant, making other memories as moonlight untQ sunlight—as water unto wine. ^

m

TO some natures security hath no charm— the sword of Damodes suspended over their heads adds to their enjoyment of an3rthing. Of such seemed Paul and his lady. It was as if they were snatching astonishing pleasures from the very brink of some danger, none the less in magnitude because unknown.

They did not breakfast until after one o'clock the next day, and then she bade him sleep—sleep on this other loggia where they sat, which gave upon the side canal obliquely, while looking into a small garden of roses and oleanders below. Here were shade and a cool small breeze.

"We are so weary, my beloved one," the lady said. "Let us sleep on these couches of smooth silk, sleep the heavy hours of the afternoon away, and go to the Piazza when the heat of the sun has lessened in measure."

m

THREE WEEKS

An immense languor was over Paul—^he asked nothing better than to rest there in the perfumed shade, near enough to his loved one to be able to stretch out his arm and touch her hair. And soon a sweet sleep claimed him, and all was oblivion and peace.

The lady lay still on her couch for a while, her eyes gleaming between their half-closed lids. But at last, when she saw that Paul indeed slept deeply, she rose stealthily and crept from the place back to the room, the gloomy vast room within, where she summoned Dmitry, and ordered the man she had called Vasili the night before into her presence. He came with cringing diffidence, prostrating himself to the ground before her, and kissing the hem of her dress, mute adoration in his dark eyes, like those of a faithful dog—a great scar showing blue on his bronzed cheek and forehead.

She questioned him imperiously, while he answered humbly in fear. Dmitry stood by, an anxious, strained look on his face, and now and then he put in a word.

Of what danger did they warn her, these two faithful servants? One came from afar for no

other purpose, it seemed. Whatever it was she received the news in haughty defiance. She spoke fiercely at first, and they humbled themselves the more. Then Anna appeared, and joined her supplications to theirs, till at last the lady, like a pettish child chasing a brood of tiresome chickens, shooed them all from the room, 'twixt laughter and tears. Then she threw up her arms in rage for a moment, and ran back to the loggia where Paul still slept. Here she sat and looked at him with burning eyes of love.

He was certainly changed in the eighteen days since she had first seen him. His face was thinner, the beautiful lines of youth were drawn with a finer hand. He was paler, too, and a shadow lay under his curly lashes. But even in his sleep it seemed as if his awakened soul had set its seal upon his expression—he had tasted of the knowledge of good and evil now.

The lady crept near him and kissed his hair. Then she flung herself on her own couch, and soon she also slept.

It was six o'clock before they awoke, Paul first —and what was his joy to be able to kneel beside her and watch her for a few seconds before her

white lids lifted themselves! An attitude of utter weariness and abandon was hers. She w^as as a child tired out with passionate weeping, who had fallen to sleep as she had flung herself do\vn. There was something even pathetic about that proud head laid low upon her clasped arms.

Paul gazed and gazed. How he worshipped her! Wayward, tigerish, beautiful Queen. But never selfish or small And what great thing had she not done for him—she who must have been able to choose from all the world a lover—and she had chosen him. How poor and narrow were all the thoughts of his former life, everywhere hedged in with foolish prejudice and ignorant certainty. Now all the world should be his lesson-book, and some day he would show her he was worthy of her splendid teaching and belief in him, and her gift of an awakened soul. He bent still lower on his knees, and kissed her feet with deepest reverence. She stirred not. She wsls so very pale—fear came to him for an instant— and then he kissed her mouth.

Her wonderful eyes unclosed themselves with none of the bewildered stare people often wake with when aroused suddenly. It seemed that even

in her sleep she had been conscious of her loved one's presence. Her lips parted in a smile, while her heavy lashes again swept her cheeks.

"Sweetheart/* she said, "you could awake me from the dead, I think. But we are living still, my Paul—waste we no more time in dreams."

They made haste, and were soon in the gondola on their way to the Piazza.

"Paul," she said, with a wave of her hand which included all the beauty around, "I am so glad you only see Venice now, when your eyes can take it in, sweetheart. At first it would have said almost nothing to you," and she smiled playfully. "In fact, my Paul would have spent most of his time in wondering how he could get exercise enough, there being so few places to walk in I He would have bought a nigger boy with a dish for his father, and some Venetian mirrors for his aunts, and perhaps—yes—a piece of Mr. Jesurum's lace for his mother, and some blown glass for his friends. He would have walked through St. Mark's, and thought it was a tumbledown place, with uneven pavements, and he would have noticed there were a 'jolly lot of pigeons' in the square! Then he would hava

THREE WEEKS

been captious with the food at his hotel, grumbled at the waiters, scolded poor Tompson—and left for Rome!"

**0h! darling!" said Paul, laughing too, in spite of his protest. **Surely, surely, I never was so bad as that—and yet I expect it is probably true. How can I ever thank you enough for giving me eyes and an understanding?"

"There—there, beloved," she said.

They walked through the Piazza; the pigeons amused Paul, and they stopped and bought corn for them, and fed the greedy creatures, ever ready for the unending largess of strangers. One or two, bolder than the rest, alighted on the lady's hat and shoulder, taking the corn from between her red lips, and Paul felt jealous even of the birds, and drew her on to see the Campanile, still standing then. They looked at it all, they looked at the lion, and finally they entered St. Mark's.

And here Paul held her arm, and gazed with bated breath. It was all so beautiful and wonderful, and new to his eyes. He had scarcely ever been in a Roman Catholic church before, and had not guessed at the gorgeous beauty of this half-Byzantine shrine. They hardly spoke. She

THREE WEEKS

did not weary him with details like a guide-book —that would be for his after-life visits—^but now he must see it just as a glorious whole.

"They worshipped here, and endowed their temple with gold and jewels," she whispered, "and then they went into the Doge's Palace, and placed a word in the lion's mouth which meant death or destruction to their best friends! A wonderful people, those old Venetians! Sly and fierce—cruel and passionate—but with ever a shrewd smile in their eye, even in their love-affairs. I often ask myself, Paul, if we are not too civilised, we of our time. We think too much of human suffering, and so we cultivate the nerves to suffer more, instead of hardening them. Picture to yourself, in my grandfather's boyhood we had still the serfs! I am of his day, though it is over—I have beaten Dmitry—"

Then she stopped speaking abruptly, as though aware she had localised her nation too much. A strange imperious expression came into her eyes as they met Paul's—almost of defiance.

Paul was moved. He began as if to speak, then he remembered his promise never to question her, and remained silent.

THREE WEEKS

*'Yes, my Paul—^you have promised, you know," she said. *'I am for you, your love—

your love—but living or dead you must never seek to know more!'*

"Ah!" he cried, "you torture me when you speak like that. Xiving or dead.' My God! that means us both—we stand or fall together."

"Dear one"—her voice fell softly into a note of intense earnestness—"while fate lets us be together—^yes—living or dead—^but if w^e must part, then either would be the cause of the death of the other by further seeking—never forget that, my beloved one. Listen"—^her eyes took a sudden fierceness—"once I read your English boc^, *The Lady and the Tiger.* You remember it, Paul ? She must choose which she would give her lover to—death and the tiger, or to another and more beautiful woman. One was left, you understand, to decide the end one's self. It caused question at the moment; some were for one choice, some for the other—but for me there was never any hesitation. I would give you to a thousand tigers sooner than to another woman— just as I would give my life a thousand times for your life, my lover."

THREE WEEKS

"Darling/- said Paul, "and I for yours, my fierce, adorable Queen. But why should we speak of terrible things? Are we not happy today, and now, and have you not told me to live while we may?"*'

"Come!" she said, and they v/alked on down to the gondola again, and floated away out to the lagoon. But when they were there, far away from the world, she talked in a new strain of earnestness to Paul. He must promise to do something with his life—something useful and great in future years.

"You must not just drift, my Paul, like so many of your countrymen do. You must help to stem the tide of your nation's decadence, and be a strong man. For me, when I read now of England, it seems as if all the hereditary legislators —it is what you call your nobles, eh ?—these men have for their motto, like Louis XV., Apres moi le deluge —It will last my time. Paul, wherever I am, it will give me joy for you to be strong and great, sweetheart. I shall know then I have not loved just a beautiful shell, whose mind I was able to light for a time. That is a sadness, Paul, perhaps the greatest of all, to see a soul one has

THREE WEEKS

illuminated and awakened to the highest point gradually slipping back to a browsing sheep, to live for la chasse alone, and horses, and dogs, with each day no higher aim than its own mean pleasure. Ah, Paul!" she continued with sudden passion, "I would rather you were dead— dead and cold with me, than I should have to feel you were growing a rien du tout —a thing who will go down into nothingness, and be forgotten by men!"

Her face was aflame with the feu sacre. The noble brow and line of her throat will ever remain in Paul's memory as a thing apart in womankind. Who couid have small or unworthy thoughts who had known her—this splendid lady?

And his worship grew and grew.

xZz

CHAPTER XVII

THAT night, as they looked from the loggia on the Grand Canal after dinner, the moonlight making things almost light as day, Dmitry begged admittance from the doorway of the great salon. The lady turned imperiously, and flashed upon him. How dared he interrupt their happy hour with things of earth?

Then she saw he was loth to speak before Paul, and that his face was grey with fear.

Paul realised the situation, and moved aside, pretending to lean from the wide windows and watch the passing gondolas, his wandering attention. However, fixing itself upon one which was moored not far from the palazzo, and occupied by a solitary figure reclining motionless in the seats. It had no coloured lights, this gondola, or merry musicians; it was just a black object of silence, tenanted by one man.

Dmitry whispered, and the lady listened, a quiver of rage going through her lithe body. Then she turned and surveyed the moored gondola, the same storm of passion and hate in her eyes as once before had come there, at the Rigi Kaltbad Belvedere.

"Shall I kill the miserable spy? Vasili would do it this night," she hissed between her clenched teeth. "But to what end ? A day's respite, perhaps, and then another, and another to face."

Dmitry raised an imploring hand to draw her from the wide arched opening, where she must be in full view of those watching below. She motioned him furiously aside, and took Paul's hand. "Come, my lover," she said, "we will look no more on this treacherous stream! It is full of the ghosts of past murders and fears. Let us return to our shrine and shut out all jars; we will sit on our tiger and forget even the moon. Beloved one—come!"

And she led him to the open doorway, but the hand which held his was cold as ice.

A tumult of emotion was dominating Paul. He understood now that danger was near—^he guessed they were being watched—^but by whom ?

By the orders of—her husband? Ah! that thought drove him mad with rage—^her husband I She—his own—the mate of his soul—of his body and soul—was the legal belonging of somebody else! Some vile man whom she hated and loathed, a "rotting carrion spoiling God's earth/' And he—Paul—^was powerless to change this fact —was powerless altogether except to love her and die for her if that would be for her good.

"Queen/* he said, his voice hoarse with passion and pain, "let us leave Venice—leave Europe altogether—let me take you av/ay to some far land of peace, and live there in safety and joy for the rest of our lives. You would always be the empress of my being and soul."

She flung herself on the tiger couch, and writhed there for some moments, burying her clenched fists in the creature's deep fur. Then she opened wide her arms, and drew Paul to her in a close, passionate embrace.

"Moi-Lioiihimyi —My beloved—^my darling one!" she whispered in anguish. "If we were lesser persons—yes, we could hide and live for a time in a tent under the stars—but we are not. They would track me, and trap us, and sooner

or later there would be the end, the ignominious, ordinary end of disgrace—" Then she clasped him closer, and whispered right m his ear m her wonderful voice, now trembling with love.

"Sweetheart—listen! Beyond all of this there is that thought, that hope, ever in my heart that one day a son of ours' shall worthily fill a throne, so we must not think of ourselves, my Paul, of the Thou, and the I, and the Now, beloved. A throne which is filled most ignobly at present, and only filled at all through my birth and my family's influence. Think not I want to plant a cheat. No! I have a right to find an heir as I will, a splendid heir who shall redeem the land—^the spirit of our two selves given being by love, and endowed by the gods. Ah! think of it, Paul. Dream of this joy and pride, it will help to still the unrest we are both suffering now. It must quiet this wild, useless rage against fate. Is it not so, my lover?"

Her voice touched his very heartstrings, but he was too deeply moved to answer her for a moment. The renewal of this thought exalted his very soul. All that was noble and great in his

nature seemed rising up in one glad triumph-song.

A son of his and hers to fill a throne! Ah! God, if that were so!

"I love the English/' she whispered. "I have known the men of all nations—but I love the English best. They are straight and just—the fine ones at least. They are brave and fair—and fearless. And our baby Paul shall be the most splendid of any. Beloved one, you must not think me a visionary—a woman dreaming of what might never be—I see it—I know it. This will come to pass as I say, and then we shall both find consolation and rest."

Thus she whispered on until Paul was intoxicated with joy and glory, and forgot time and place and danger and possible parting. A host of triumphant angels seemed singing in his ears. Then she read him poetry, and let him caress her, and smiled in his arms.

But towards morning, if he had awakened, he would have found his lady prostrate with silent weeping. The intense concentrated grief of a strong nature taking its farewell

CHAPTER XVIII

OW this Thursday was the night of the full moon. A cloudless morning sky promised a glorious evening. The lovers woke early, and had their breakfast on the loggia overlooking the oleander garden. The lady w^as in an enchanting mood of sunshine, and no one could have guessed of the sorrow of her dawn vigil thoughts. She was wayward and playful—one moment petting Paul with exquisite sweetness, the next teasing his curls and biting the lobes of his ears. She never left him for one second—it seemed she must teach him still more subtle caresses, and call forth even new shades of emotion and bliss. All fear was banished, only a brilliant glory remained. She laughed and half-closed her eyes with provoking smiles. She undulated about, creeping as a ser-

pent over her lover, and kissing his eyelids and hair. They were so infinitely happy it was growing to afternoon before they thought of leaving their loggia, and then they started in the open gondola, and glided away through quaint, narrow canals until they came to the lagoon.

"We shall not stay in the gondola long, my Paul," she said. "I cannot bear to be out of your arms, and our palace is fair. And oh! my beloved, to-night I shall feast you as never before. The night of our full moon! Paul, I have ordered a bower of roses and music and song. I want you to remember it the whole of your life."

"As though I could forget a moment of our time, my sweet," said Paul. "It needs no feasts or roses—only whatever delights you to do, delights me too."

"Paul," she cooed after a while, during which her hand had lain in his and there had been a soft silence, "is not this a life of joy, so smooth and gliding, this way of Venice? It seems far from ruffles and storms. I shall love it always, shall not you? and you must come back in other years and study its buildings and its history, Paul—with your new, fine eyes."

"We shall come together, my darling," he answered. "I should never want anything alone."

"Sweetheart!" she cooed again in his ears; and then presently, "Paul," she said, "some day you must read 'Salammbo,' that masterpiece of Flaubert's. There is a spirit of love in that which now you would understand—^the love which looked out of Matho's eyes when his body was beaten to jelly. It is the love I have for you, my own— 2l love *beyond all words or sense'—^as one of your English poets says. Do you know, with the strange irony of things, when a woman's love for a man rises to the highest point there is in it always an element of the wife? However wayward and tigerish and imdomestic she may be, she then desires to be the acknowledged possession and belonging of the man, even to her own dishonour. She desires to reproduce his likeness, she wants to compass his material good. She will think of his food, and his raiment, and his well-being, and never of her own—only, if she is wise she will hide all these things in her heart, for the average man cannot stand this great light of

her sweetness, and when her love becomes selfless, his love will wane."

"The average man's—^yes, perhaps so," agreed Paul. "But then, what does the average person of either sex know of love at all?"

"They think they know," she said. "Really think it, but love like ours happens perhaps once in a century, and generally makes history of some sort—^bad or good."

"Let it!" said Paul. "I am like Antony in that poem you read me last night. I must have you for my own, *Though death, dishonour, anything you will, stand in the way.' He knew 'A^hat he was talking about, Antony! so did the man who wrote the poem!"

"He was a great sculptor as well as a poet," the lady said. "And yes, he knew all about those wonderful lovers better far than your Shakespeare did, who leaves me quite cold when I read his view of them. Cleopatra was to me so subtle, so splendid a queen."

"Of course she was just you, my heart," said Paul. "You are her soul living over again, and that poem you must give me to keep some day, because it says just what I shall want to say if

ever I must be away from you for a time. See, have I remembered it right ?

" Tell her, till I see Those eyes, I do not live—^that Rome to me Is hateful,—tell her— oh!—I know not what—• That every thought and feeling, space and spot, Is like an ugly dream where she is not; All persons plagues; all living wearisome; All talking empty . . /'

"Yes, that is what I should say—I say it to myself now even in the short while I am absent from you dressing !'*

The lady's eyes brimmed with tenderness. *Taul!—^you do love me, my own!" she said.

*'0h, why can't we go on and travel together, darling?" Paul continued. *T want you to show me the world—at least the best of Europe. In every country you would make me feel the spirit of the place. Let us go to Greece, and see the temples and worship those old gods. They knew about love, did they not?"

The lady leant back and smiled, as if she liked to hear him talk.

tt2a

"I often ask myself did they really know," she said. "They knew the whole material part of it at any rate. They were perhaps too practical to have indulged in the mental emotions we weave into it now—but they were wise, they did not educate the wives and daughters, they realised that to perform well domestic duties a woman's mind should not be over-trained in learning. Learning and charm and grace of mind were for the others, the hetcercB of whom they asked no tiresome ties. And in all ages it is unfortunately not the simple good women who have ruled the hearts of men. Think of Pericles and Aspasia— Antony and Cleopatra—^Justinian and Theodora —Belisarius and Antonina—and later, all the mistresses of the French kings—even, too, your English Nelson and Lady Hamilton! Not one of these was a man's ideal of what a wife and mother ought to be. So no doubt the Greeks were right in that principle, as they were right in all basic principles of art and balance. And now we mix the whole thing up, my Paul— \ domesticity and learning—nerves and art, and feverish cravings for the impossible new—so we

get a conglomeration of false proportions, and a ceaseless unrest/'

"Yes," said Paul, and thought of his mother. She was a perfectly domestic and beautiful woman, but somehow he felt sure she had never made his father's heart beat. Then his mind went back to the argument in what the lady had said—he wanted to hear more.

"If this is so, that would prove that all the very clever women of history were immoral—do you mean that?" he asked.

The lady laughed.

"Immoral! It is so quaint a word, my Paul! Each one sees it how they will. For me it is immoral to be false, to be mean, to steal, to cheat, to stoop to low actions and small ends. Yet one can be and do all those things, and if one remains as well the faithful beast of burden to one man, one is counted in the world a moral woman! But that shining light of hypocrisy and virtue— to judge by her sentiments in her writings—^your George Eliot, must be classed as immoral because, having chosen her mate without the law's bless- \ ing, she yet wrote the highest sentiments of British respectability! To me she was being immoral

only because she was deliberately doing what—» again I say, judging by her writings— she felt must be a grievous wrong. That is immoral— deliberately to still one's conscience and indulge in a pleasure against it. But to live a life with one's love, if it engenders the most lofty aspirations, to me is highly moral and good. I feel myself ennobled, exalted, because you are my lover, and our child, when it comes to us, will have a noble mind."

The thought of this, as ever, made Paul thrill; he forgot all other arguments, and a quiver ran through him of intense emotion; his eyes swam and he clasped more tightly her hand. The lady, too, leant back and closed her eyes.

"Oh! the beautiful dream!" she said, "the beautiful, beautiful—certainly! Sweetheart, let us have done with all this philosophising and go back to our palace, where we are happy in the temple of the greatest of all Gods—^the God of Love!"

Then she gave the order for home.

But on the way they stopped at Jesurum's, and she supervised Paul's purchases for his mother, and allowed him to buy herself some small gifts.

^Aiid between them they spent a gCMDd (leal of money, and laughed over it like happy children. So when they got back to the palazzo there was joy in their hearts like the sunlight of the late afternoon. !

She would not let Paul go on to the loggia overlooking the Grand Canal. He had noticed as they passed that some high screens of lilac-bushes had been placed in front of the wide arched openings. No fear of prying eyes from opposite houses now! And yet they were not too high to prevent those in the loggia from seeing the moon and the sky. Their feast was preparing evidently, ^nd he knew it would be a night of the gods.

But from then until it was time to dress for dinner his lady decreed that they should rest in their rooms.

"Thou must sleep, my Paul," she said, "so that thy spirit may be fresh for new joys."

And it was only after hard pleading she would allow him to have it that they rested on the other loggia couches, so that his closing eyes might know hf^x near.

CHAPTER XIX

NO Englishwoman would have thougHt of the details which made the Feast of the Full Moon so wonderful in Paul's eyes. It savoured rather of other centuries and the days of Imperial Rome, and indeed, had his lady been one of Britain's daughters, he too might have found it a little bizarre. As it was, it was all in the note—the exotic note of Venice and her spells.

The lady had gone to her room wlTen lie woke on the loggia, and he had only time to dress before the appointed moment when he was to meet her in the little salon.

She was seated on the old Venetian chair she had bought in Lucerne when Paul entered—the most radiant vision he had yet seen. Her garment was pale-green gauze. It seemed to cling in misty folds round her exquisite shape; it was

THREE WEEKS

clasped with pearls; the most magnificent ones hung in a row round her throat and fell from her ears. A diadem confined her glorious hair, which descended in the two long strands twisted with chains of emeralds and diamonds. Her whole personality seemed breathing magnificence and panther-like grace. And her eyes glowed with passion, and mystery, and force.

Paul knelt like a courtier, and kissed her hand. Then he led her to their feast.

Dmitry raised the curtain of the loggia door as they approached, and what a sight met PauFs view!

The whole place had been converted into a bower of roses. The walls were entirely covered with them. A great couch of deepest red ones was at one side, fixed in such masses as to be quite resisting and firm. From the roof chains of roses hung, concealing small lights—while from above the screen of lilac-bushes in full bloom the moon in all her glory mingled with the rose-shaded lamps and cast a glamour and unreality over the whole.

The dinner was laid on a table in the centre, and the table was covered with tuberoses and

THREE WEEKS

stephanotis, surrounding the cupid fountain of perfume. The scent of all these flowers! And the warm summer night! . No wonder Paul's senses quivered with exaltation. No wonder his head swam.

They had scarcely been seated when from the great salon, whose open doors were hidden by falling trellises of roses, there came the exquisite sounds of violins, and a boy's plaintive voice. A concert of all sweet airs played softly to further excite the sense. Paul had not thought such musicians could be obtained in Venice, and guessed, and rightly, that, like the cook and the artist who had designed it, they hailed from Paris, to beautify this night.

Throughout the repast his lady bewildered him with her wild fascination. Never before had she seemed to collect all her moods into one subtle whole, cemented together by passionate love. It truly was a night of the gods, and the exaltation of Paul's spirit had reached its zenith.

"My Paul," she said, when at last only the rare fruits and the golden wine remained, and ihey were quite alone—even the musicians had retired, and their airs floated up from a gondola

THREE WEEKS

below. "My Paul, I want you never to forget (this night—never to think of me but as gloriously happy, clasped in your arms amid the roses. And see, we must drink once more together of our wedding wine, and complete our souls' delight.'*

An eloquence seemed to come to Paul and loosen his tongue, so that he whispered back paeans of worship in language as fine as her own. And the moon flooded the loggia with her light, and the roses gave forth their scent. It was the supreme effort of art and nature to cover them with glorious joy.

"My darling one," the lady whispered in his ear, as she lay in his arms on the couch of roses, crushed deep and half buried in their velvet leaves, "this is our souls' wedding. In life and in death they can never part more."

Dawn was creeping through the orchid blinds of their sleeping chamber when this strange Queen disengaged herself from her lover's embrace, and bent over him, kissing his young curved lips. He stirred not—the languor of utter prostration was upon him, and held him in

its grasp. In the uncertain light his sleep looked pale as death.

The lady gazed at him, an anguish too deep for tears in her eyes. For was not this the end—■ the very end ? Fierce, dry sobs shook her. There was something terrible and tigerish in her grief. And yet her will made her not linger—^there was still one thing to do.

She rose and turned to the writing-table by the window, then drawing the blind aside a little she began rapidly to write. When she had finished, without reading the missive over, she went and placed it with a flat leather jewel-case on her pillow beside Paul. And soon she commenced a madness of farewells—all restrained and gentle for fear he should awake.

"My love, my love,*' she wailed between her kisses, "God keep you safe—though He may never bring you back to me."

Then with a wild, strangled sob, she fled from the room.

SOB

CHAPTER X^

A HUSH was over everything wfien Paul first awoke—^the hush of a hot, drowsy noontide.

He stretched out his arm to touch his loved one, as was his custom, to draw her near and envelop her with caresses and greeting—^an instinct which came to him while yet half asleep.

But his arm met empty space. What was this? He opened his eyes wide and sat up in bed. He was alone—where had she gone? He had slept so late, that was it. She was playing one of her sweet tricks upon him. Perhaps she was even hiding behind the curtain which covered the entrance to the side loggia where they were accustomed to breakfast. He would look and see. He rose quickly and lifted the heavy drapery. No—^the loggia was untenanted, and breakfast was laid for one! That was the first chill-^for one! Was she angry at his drowsi-

ness? Good God! what could it mean? He staggered a little, and sat on the bed, clutching the fine sheet. And as he did so it disclosed the letter and the flat leather case, which had fallen from the pillow and become hidden in the clothes.

A deadly faintness :ame over Paul. For a few seconds he trembled so his shaking fingers refused to hold the paper. Then with a mighty effort he mastered himself, and tearing the envelope open began to read.

It was a wonderful letter. The last passionate cry of her great loving heart. It passed in review their glorious days in burning words—from the first moment of their meeting. And then, towards the end, "My Paul," she wrote, "that first night you were my caprice, and afterwards my love, but now you are my life, and for this I must leave you, to save that life, sweet lover. Seek me not, heart of my heart. Believe me, I would not go if there were any other way. Fate is too strong for us, and I must bow my head. Were I to remain even another hour, all Dmitry's watching could not keep you safe. Darling, while I thought they menaced me alone, it only angered me, but now I know that you would pay the penalty, I can but go. If you follow me, it will mean death for us both. Oh! Paul, I implore you, by our great love, go into safety as soon as you can. You must leave Venice, and return straight to England, and your home. Darling—^beloved—lover—if we never meet again in this sad world let this thought stay with you always, that I love you—^heart and mind— body and soul—I am utterly and forever Yours." ^ As he read the last words the room became dark for Paul, and he fell back like a log on the bed, the paper fluttering to the floor from his nerveless fingers.

She was gone—and life seemed over for him.

Here, perhaps an hour later, Tompson found him still unconscious, and in terrified haste sent off for a doctor, and telegraphed to Sir Charles Verdayne:

*'Come at once,

Tompson.'^'

But ere his father could arrive on Sunday, Paul was lying 'twixt life and death, madly raving with brain fever.

t And thus ended the three weeks of his episode.

CHAPTER XXI

HAVE any of you who read crept back to life fron. nearly beyond the grave? Crept back to find it shorn of all that made it fair? After hours of delirium to awaken in great weakness to a sense of hideous anguish and loss—to the prospect of days of aching void and hopeless longing, to the hourly, momentary sting of remembrance of things vaster than death, more dear than life itself? If you have come through this valley of the shadow, then you can know what the first days of returning consciousness meant to Paul.

He never really questioned the finality of her decree, he sensed it meant parting for ever. And yet, with that spring of eternal hope which animates all living souls, unbidden arguings and possibilities rose in his enfeebled brain, and deepened his unrest. Thus his progress towards convalescence was long and slow.

J20S

And all this time his father and Tompson had liUrsed him in the old Venetian palazzo with ten-derest devotion.

The Italian servants had been left, paid tip for a month, but the lady and her Russian retinue had vanished, leaving no trace.

Both Tompson and Sir Charles knew almost the whole story now from FauF's ravings, and neither spoke of it—except that Tompson supplied some links to complete Sir Charles' picture.

"She was the most splendid lady you could wish to see, Sir Charles," the stolid creature finished with. "Her servants worshipped her— and if Mr. Verdayne is ill now, he is ill for no less than a Queen.'-

This fact comforted Tompson greatly, but Paul's father found in it no consolation.

The difficulty had been to prevent his mother from descending upon them. She must ever be kept in ignorance of this episode in her son's life. She belonged to the class of intellect which could never have understood. It would have been an undying shock and horrified grief to the end of her life—excellent, loving, conventional lady!

So after the first terrible danger was over, Sir

Charles made light of their son's illness. Paul and he were enjoying Venice, he said, and would soon be home. "D—d hard luck the boy getting fever like this!'* he wrote in his laconic style, "but one never could trust foreign countries* drains!"

!A.nd the Lady Henrietta waited in unsuspecting, well-bred patience.

iThose were weary days for every one concerned. It wrung his father's heart to see Paul prostrate there, as weak as an infant. All his splendid youth and strength conquered by this raging blast. It was sad to have to listen to his ever-constant moan:

"Darling, come back to me—darling, my Queen."

. And even after he regained consciousness, it was equally pitiful to watch him lying nerveless and white, blue shadows on his once fresh skin. And most pitiful of all were his hands, now veined and transparent, falling idly upon the sheet.

But at least the father realised it could have been no ordinary woman whose going caused the shock which—even after a life of three weeks'

continual emotion—could prostrate his young Hercules. She must have been worth something '—this tiger Queen.

And one day, contrary to his usual custom, he addressed Tompson:

"What sort of a looking woman, Tompson?"

And Tompson, although an English valet, did not reply, "Who, Sir Charles ?"—he just rounded his eyes stolidly and said in his monotonous voice:

"She was that forcible-looking, a man couldn^t say when he got close, she kind of dazzled him. She had black hair, and a white face, and—^and— witch's eyes, but she was very kind and overpowering, haughty and generous. Any one would have known she was a Queen."

"Young?" asked Sir Charles.

Tompson smoothed his chin: "I could not say, Sir Charles. Some days about twenty-five, and other days past thirty. About thirty-three to thirty-five, I expect she was, if the truth were known."

"Pretty?"

The eyes rounded more and more. "Well, she was 30 fascinatiu', I can't say, Sir Charles— the

most lovely lady I ever did see at times, Sir Charles/*

"Humph," said PauFs father, and then relapsed into silence.

"She'd a beast of a husband; he might have been a King, but he was no gentleman," Tompson ventured to add presently, fearing the "Humph" perhaps meant disapprobation of this splendid Queen. "Her servants were close, and did not speak good English, so I could not get much out of them, but the man Vasili, who came the last days, did say in a funny lingo, which I had to guess at, as how he expected he should have to kill him some time. Vasili had a scar on his face as long as your finger that he'd got defending the Queen from her husband's brutalit)', when he was the worse for drink, only last year. And Mr. Verdayne is so handsome. It is no wonder, Sir Charles—"

"That will do, Tompson," said Sir Charles, and he frowned.

The fatal letter, carefully sealed up in a new envelope, and the leather case were in his despatch-box. Tompson had handed tlicm to him on his arrival. And one day when Paul appeared well enough to be lifted into a long chair on the side loggia, his father thought fit to give them to him.

Paul's apathy seemed paralysing. The days had passed, since the little Italian doctor had pronounced him out of danger, in one unending languid quietude. He expressed interest in no single thing. He was polite, and indifferent, and numb.

*'He must be roused now," Sir Charles said to the doctor. "It is too hot for Venice, he must be moved to higher air/' and the little man had nodded his head.

So this warm late afternoon^ as he lay under the mosquito curtains—^w^hich the coming of June had made necessary in this paradise—his father said to him:

"I have a letter and a parcel of yours, Paul: you had better look at them—we hope to start north in a day or two—you must get to a more bracing place."

Then he had pushed them under the net-folds, and turned his back on the scene.

The blood rushed to Paul's face, but left him deathly pale after a few moments. And presently

THREE WEEKS

he broke the seal. Ths minute Sphinx in the corner of the paper seemed to mock at him. Indeed, Hfe was a riddle of pnguish and pain. He read the letter all over—and read it again. The passionate words of love warmed him now that he had passed the agony of the farewell. One sentence he had hardly grasped before, in particular held balm. "Sweetheart,^' it said, "you must not grieve—think always of the future and of our hope. Our love is not dead with our parting, and one day there will be the living sign—'* Yes, that thought w<is comfort—but how should he know ?

Then he turned to the leather case. His fingers were still so feeble that with difficulty he pressed the spring to open it.

He glanced up at his father's distinguished-looking back outlined against the loggia's opening arches. It appeared uncompromising. A fixed determination to stare at the oleanders below seemed the only spirit animating this parent.

Yes—^he must open the box. It gave suddenly with a jerk, and there lay a dog's collar, made of small flexible plates of pure beaten gold, mounted on Russian leather, all of the finest workmanship.

THREE WEEKS

And on a slip of paper in his darling*s own writing he read:

'*This is for Pike, my beloved one; let him wear it ahvays—^a gift from me."

On the collar itself, finely engraved, were the words, *Tike, belonging to Paul Verdayne."

Then the floodgates of Paul's numbed soul were opened, a great sob rose in his breast. He covered his face with his hands, and cried like a child.

Oh! her dear thought! her dear, tender thought ^for Pike! His little friend!

And Sir Charles made believe he saw nothing, as he stole from the place, his rugged face twitching a little, and his keen eyes dim.

'ZIZ

CHAPTER XXri

r I 1 HEY did not go north, as Sir Charles intended, an unaccountable reluctance on Paul's part to return through Switzerland changed their plans. Instead, by a fortunate chance, the large schooner yacht of a rather eccentric old friend came in to Venice, and the father eagerly acccepted the invitation to go on board and bring his invalid.

The owner, one Captain Grigsby, had been quite alone, so the three men would be in peace, and nothing could be better for Paul than this warm, sea air.

"Typhoid fever?" Mark Grigsby had asked.

"No," Sir Charles had replied, "considerable mental tribulation over a woman." >

"D—d kittle cattle!" was Captain Grigsby^s polite comment. "A fine boy, too, and promising—"

THREE WEEKS

"Appears to have been almost worth while,** Sir Charles added, "from what I gather— and, confound it, Grig, we'd have done the same in our day."

But Captain Grigsby only repeated: "D—d kittle cattle!"

And so they weighed anchor, and sailed along the Italian shores of the sun-lit Adriatic.

These were better days for Paul. Each hour brought him back some health and vigour. Youth and strength w^ere asserting their own again, and the absence of familiar objects, and the glory of the air and the blue sea helped sometimes to deaden the poignant agony of his aching heart. But there it was underneath, an ever-present, dull anguish. And only when he became sufficiently strong to help the sailors with the ropes, and exert physical force, did he get one moment's respite. The two elder men watched him with kind, furtive eyes, but they never questioned him, or made the slightest allusion to his travels.

And the first day they heard him laugh Sir Charles looked down at the white foam because a mist was in his eyes.

They had coasted round Italy and Sicily, and

THREE WEEKS

not among the Ionian Isles, as had been Captain Grigsby's intention.

"I fancy the lady came from some of those Balkan countries/' Sir Charles had said. "Don't Jet us get in touch with even the outside of one of them."

And Mark Grigsby had grunted an assent.

"The boy is a fine fellow," he said one morning as they looked at Paul hauling ropes. "He'll probably never get quite over this, but he is fighting like a man, Charles—tell me as much as you feel inclined to of the story."

So Sir Charles began in his short, broken sentences :

"Parson's girl to start with—sympathy over a broken collar-bone. The wife behaved unwisely about it, so the boy thought he was in love. We sent him to travel to get rid of that idea. It appears he met this lady in Lucerne—seems to have been an exceptional person—a Russian, Tompson says—a Queen or Princess incog., the fellow tells me—but I can't spot her as yet. Hubert will know who she was, though—^but it does not matter—the woman herself was the

THREE WEEKS

jthing. Gather she was quite a remarkable woman —ten years older than Paul."

"Always the case," growled Captain Grigsby.

Sir Charles puffed at his pipe—and then: **They were only together three weeks," he said. **And during that time she managed to cram more knowledge of everything into the boy's head than you and I have got in a lifetime. Give you my word. Grig, when he was off his chump in the fever, he raved like a poet, and an orator, and he was only an ordinary sportsman when he left home in the spring! Cleopatra, he called her one day, and I fancy that was the ke^niote—she must have been one of those exceptional women we read of in the sixth form."

"And fortunately never met!" said Captain Grigsby.

"I don't know," mused Sir Charles. "It might have been good to live as wildly even at the price. We've both been about the wprld. Grig, since the days we fastened on our cuirasses together for the first time, and each thought himself the devil of a fine fellow—^but I rather doubt if we now know as much of what is really worth

THREE WEEKS

having as my boy there—just twenty-tHree years old."

"Nonsense!" snapped Captain Grigsby—but there was a tone of regret in his protest.

"Lucky to have got off without a knife or a bullet through him—dangerous nations to grapple with," he said.

"Yes—I gather some pretty heavy menace was over their heads, and that is what made the lady decamp, so we've much to be thankful for," agreed Sir Charles.

"Had she any children ?" the other asked.

"Tompson says no. Rotten fellow the husband, it appears, and no heir to the throne, or principality, or whatever it is—sO' when I have had a talk with Hubert—Henrietta's brother, you know—the one in the Diplomatic Service, it will be easy to locate her—gathered Paul doesn't know himself."

"Pretty romance, anyway. And what will you do with the boy now, Charles ?"

Paul's father puffed quite a long while at his meerschaum before he answered, and then his voice was gruffer than ever with tenderness suppressed,

THREE WEEKS

"Give him his head, Grig," he said. "He's true blue underneath, and he'll come up to the collar in time, oLd friend—only I shall have to keep his mother's love from harrying him. Best and greatest lady in the world, my wife, but she's rather apt to jog the bridle now and then."

At this moment Paul joined them. His paleness showed less than usual beneath the sunburn, and his eyes seemed almost bright. A wave of thankful gladness filled his father's heart.

"Thank God," he said, below his breath. "Thank God."

The weather had been perfection, hardly a drop of rain, and just the gentlest breezes to waft them slowly along. A suitable soothing idle life for one who had but lately been near death. And each day Paul's strength returned, until his father began to hope they might still be home for his birthday the last day of July. They had crept up the coast of Italy now, when an absolute calm fell upon them, and just opposite the temple of P^stum they decided to anchor for the night.

For the last evenings, as the moon had grown larger, Paul had been strangely restless. It seemed as if he preferred to tire himself out witH

THREE WEEKS

unnecessary rope-pulling, and then retire to his berth the moment that dinner was over, rather than go on deck. His face, too, which had been controlled as a mask until now, wore a look of haunting anguish which was grievous to see. He ate his dinner—or rather, pretended to play with the food—in absolute silence.

Uneasiness overcame Sir Charles, and he glanced at his old friend. But Paul, after lighting a cigar, and letting it out once or twice, rose, and murmuring something about the heat, went up on deck.

It was the night of the full moon—eight weeks exactly since the joy of life had finished for him.

He felt he could not bear even the two kindly gentlemen whose unspoken sympathy he knew was his. He could not bear anything human. To-night, at least, he must be alone with his grief.

All nature was in a mood divine. They were close enough inshore to see the splendid temples clearly with the naked eye. The sky and the sea were of the colour only the Mediterranean knows. It was hot and still, and the moon in her pure magnificence cast her never-ending spell.

Not a sound of the faintest ripple met his ear.

THREE WEEKS

The sailors supped below. All was silence. 0:i one side the vast sea, on the other the shore, with this masterpiece of man's genius, the temple of the great god Poseidon, in this vanished settlement of the old Greeks. How marvellously beautiful it all was, and how his Queen would have loved it! How she would have told him its history and woven round it the spirit of the past, until his living eyes could almost have seen the priests and the people, and heard their worshipping prayers! \

His darling had spoken of it once, he remembered, and had told him it was a place they must see. He recollected her very words:

"We must look at it first in the winter from the shore, my Paul, and see those splendid proportions outlined against the sky—so noble and so perfectly balanced—and then we must see it from the sea, with the background of the olive hills. It is ever silent and deserted and calm, and death lurks there after the month of March. A cruel malaria, which we must not face, dear love. But if we could, we ought to see it from a yacht in safety in the summer time, and then the sgell would fall upon us, and we would know

THREE WEEKS

it was true tHat rose-trees really grew tKere whictt gave the world their blossoms twice a year. That was the legend of the Greeks."

Well, he was seeing it from a yacht, but ah, God! seeing it alone—alone. And where was i So intense and vivid was his remembrance of her that he could feel her presence near. If he turned his head, he felt he should see her standing beside him, her strange eyes full of love. iThe very perfume of her seemed to fill the air— her golden voice to whisper in his ear—^her soul to mingle with his soul. Ah yes, in spirit, as she had said, they could never be parted more. .

A suppressed moan of anguish escaped his lips, and his father, who had come silently behind him, j)ut his hand on his arm.

"My poor boy," he ?aid, his gruff voice Hoarse in his throat, "if only to God I could do something for you!"

"Oh, father!" said Paul.

And the two men looked in each other's eyes, and knew each other as never before.

35 1 ?K * ^ *: Hf

'22l\

N

CHAPTER XXIir

EXT day there was a fresh breeze, and they scudded before it on to Naples. Here Paul seemed well enough to take train, and so arrive in England in time for his birthday. He owed this to his mother, he and his father both felt. She had been looldng forward to it for so long, as at the time of his coming of age the festivities had been interrupted by the sudden death of his maternal grandfather, and the people had all been promised a continuance of them on this, his twenty-third birthday. So, taking the journey by sufficiently easy stages, sleeping three nights on the way, they calculated to arrive on the eve of the event.

The Lady Henrietta would have everything in readiness for them, and her darling Paul was not to be over-hurried. Only guests of the most congenial kind had been invited, and such a number of nice girls!

THREE WEEKS

The prospect was perfectly delightful, and ought to cause any young man pure joy.

It was with a heart as heavy as lead Paul mounted the broad steps of his ancestral home that summer evening, and was folded in his mother's arms. (The guests were all fortunately dressing for dinner.)

Captain Grigsby had been persuaded to abandon his yacht and accompany them too.

"Yes, I'll come, Charles," he said. "Getting too confoundedly hot in these seas; besides, the boy will want more than one to see him through among those cackling vv^omen."

So the three had travelled together through Italy and France—Switzerland had been strictly avoided.

"Paul! darling!" his mother exclaimed, in a voice of pained surprise as she stood back and looked at him. "But surely you have been very ill. My darling, darling son—"

"I told you he had had a sharp attack of fever, Henrietta," interrupted Sir Charles quickly, "and no one looks their best after travelling in this grilling weather. Let the boy get to his bath, and you will see a different person."

THREE WEEKS

But his mother's loving eyes were not to Ke deceived. So with infinite fuss, and terms of endearment, she insisted upon accompanying her offspring to his room, where the dignified housekeeper was summoned, and his every imaginable and unimaginable want arranged to be supplied.

Once all this would have irritated Paul to the verge of bearish rudeness, but now he only kissed his mother's white jewelled hand. He remembered his lady's tender counsel to him, given in one of their many talks: "You must always reverence your mother, Paul, and accept her worship with love.'* So now he said:

"Dear mother, it is so good of you, but I'm all right—fever does knock one over a bit, you know. You'll see, though, being at home again will make me perfectly well in no time—and I'll be as good as you like, and eat and drink all Mrs. Elwyn's beef-teas and jellies, and other beastly stuff, if you will just let me dress now, like a darling.'*

However, his mother was obliged to examine and assure herself that his beautiful hair was still thick and waving—and she had to pause and sigh over every sharpened line of his face and figure —^though the thought of being permitted to lavish

THREE WEEKS

continuous care for long days to come held a certain consolation for her.

At last Paul was left alone, and there came a moment he had been longing* for. He had sent written orders that Tremlett should bring Pike, and leave him in his dressing-room beyond— and all the while his mother had talked he had heard suppressed whines and scratchings. Somehow he had not wanted to see his dog before any of the people; the greeting between himself and his little friend must be in solitude, for was there not a secret link between them in that golden collar given by his Queen ?

And Pike would understand—^he certainly would understand!

If short, passionate barks, and a madness of wagging tail-stump, accompanied by jumps of crazy joy, could comfort any one—^then Paul had his full measure when the door was opened, and this rough white terrier bounded in upon him, and, frantic with welcome and ecstasy, was with difficulty quieted at last in his master's fond arms.

"Oh! Pike, Pike!" Paul said, while tears of weakness flowed down his cheeks. "I can talk

to you—^and when you wear her collar you will know my Queen—our Queen."

And Pike said everything of sympathy a dog could say. But it was not until late at night, when the interminable evening had been got through, that his master had the pleasure of trying his darling's present on.

That first evening of his homecoming was an ordeal for Paul. He was still feeble, and dead tired from travelling, to begin with—and to have to listen and reply to the endless banalities of his mother's guests was almost more than he could bear.

'. They were a nice cHeery company of mostly young friends. Pretty girls and his own boon companions abounded, and they chaffed and played silly games after dinner—until Paul could have groaned.

.,' Captain Grigsby Had eventually caught Sir Charles' eye:

' *^ou will have the boy fainting if you don't get him off alone soon," he said. "These girls would tire a man in strong health!"

And at last Paul had escaped to his own room.

He leant out of his window, and looked at the

gibbous moon. Pike was there on the broad sill beside him, under his arm, and he could feel the golden collar on the soft fur neck—a wave of perhaps the most hopeless anguish he had yet felt was upon his spirit now. The unutterable blankness—the impossible vista of the endless days to come, with no prospect of meeting—^no aim—^no hope. Yes, she had said there was one hope—one hope which could bring peace to their crueJ unrest. But how and when should he eve?: know ? And if it were so—then more than ever he should be by her side. The number of beautiful things he would want to say to her about it all—^the oceans of love he would desire to pour upon her—the tender care whicH should be his hourly joy. To honour and worship her, and chase all pain away. And he did not even know her name, or the country where one day this hope should reign. That was incredible—and it would be so easy to find out. But he had promised her never to make inquiries, and he would keep his word. He saw her reason now; It had arisen in an instinct of tender protection for himself. She had known if he knew her place of abode no fear of death would keep him from trying to see her.

AH1 he Kad had the tears—and why not the cold steel and blood ? It was no price to pay could he but hear once more her golden voice, and feel her loving, twining arms.

He was only held back by the fear of the dagger for her. And instead of being with her, and waiting on her footsteps, he should have to spend his next hours with those ridiculous Englishwomen ! Those foolish, flippant girls! One had quoted poetry to him at dinner, the very scrap his lady had spoken a line of—this new poet's, who was taking the world of London by storm that year: "Loved with a love beyond all words or sense!'* And it had sounded like bathos or sacrilege. What did these dolls know of love, or life? Chattering parrots to weary a man's brain! Yes, the Greeks were right, it would be better to keep them spinning flax, and uneducated.

An3 so in his young intolerance, maddened by pain, he saw all things gibbous like the mocking moon. Pike stirred under his arm and licked his hand, a faint whine of love making itself heard in the night.

•*0 God!" said Paul, as he buried his face in

Bis Hands, "let me get through this time as she would have me do; let me not show the anguish in my heart, but be at least a man and gentle-

man."

m ^ ^

CHAPTER XXIV

THE neighbours and his parents were astonished at the eloquence of Paul's speech at the great dinner given to the tenants next day. No one had guessed at his powers before, and the county papers, and indeed some London reporters, had predicted a splendid political future for this young orator. It had been quite a long speech, and contained sound arguments and common sense, and was expressed in language so lofty and refined that it sent ecstatic admiration through his miOther's fond breast.

And all the time Paul spoke he saw no sea of faces below him—only his soul's eyes were looking into those strange chameleon orbs of his lady. He said every word as if she had been there, and at the end it almost seemed she must have heard him, so soft a peace fell on his spirit. Yes, she would have been pleased with her lover, he knew, and that held large grains of consoktion.

And so these days passed in well-accomplisHe9 duty; and at last all the festivities were over, and he could rest.

Captain Grigsby and his father had helped him v^henever they could, and an eternal bond of friendship was cemented between the three.

"By Jove, Charles! You ought to be thundering proud of that boy!" Captain Grigsby said the morning of his departure for Scotland on August lo. "He's come up to the scratch like a hero, and whatever the damage, the lady must have been well worth while to turn him out polished like that. Gad! Charles, I'd take a month's journey to see her myself."

And Paul's father grunted witH satisfaction as he said: "I told you so."

Thus the summer days went by in the strengthening of Paul's character—^trying always to live up to an ideal—^trying ever to dominate his grief —but never trying to forget.

By the autumn shooting time his health was quite restored, and except that he looked a year or so older there were no outward traces of the passing through that valley of the shadow, from whence he had escaped with just his life.

But the three weeks of his lady's influence had changed the inner man beyond all recognition. His spirit was stamped with her nameless distinction, and all the vistas she had opened for liim to the tree of knowledge he now followed up. No smallest incident of his day seemed unconnected with some thought or wish of hers—so that in truth she still guided and moulded him by the power of her great soul.

But in spite of all these things, the weeks and months held hours of aching longing and increasing anxiety to know how she fared. If she should be ill. If their hope was coming true, then now she must be suffering, and suffering all alone. Sometimes tlie agony of the thought was more than Paul could bear, and cook him off with Pike alone into the leafless woods which crowned a hill at the top of the park. And then he would pause, and look out at the view, and the dull November sky, a madness of agonising unrest torturing his heart.

The one thing he felt glad of was the absence of his Uncle Hubert, who had been made Minister in a South American Republic, and would not return to England for more than a year.

So

there would be no temptation to question him, or perchance to hear one of his clever, evil jests which might contain some allusion to his lady. Lord Hubert Aldringham was fond of boasting of his royal acquaintances, and was of a mind that found "not even Lancelot brave, nor Galahad clean." Now all Paul could do was to wait and hope. At least his Queen had his address. She could write to him, even though he could not write to her—^and surely, surely, some news of her must come.

Thus the winter arrived, and the hunting— hunting that he had been sure was what he liked best in all the world.

And now it just served to pass the time and distract some hours from the anguishing ache by its physical pleasure. But in that, as in everything he did at this time, Paul tried to outshine his fellows, and gain one more laurel to lay at the feet of his Queen. Socially he was having an immense success. He began to be known as some one worth listening to by men, and women hung on his w^ords. It was peculiarly delightful to find so young and beautiful a creature with all the knowledge and fascinating cachet of a man

of the world. And then his complete indifference to them piqued and allured them still more. Always polite and chivalrous, but as aloof as a mountain top. Paul had no small vanity to be soothed by their worship into forgetting for one moment his Queen. So his shooting-visits passed, and his experience of life grew.

Isabella had returned at Christmas, engaged to a High Church curate, and beaming with satisfaction and health. And it gave Paul, and indeed them both, pleasure to meet and talk for an hour. She was a good sort always, and if he marvelled to himself how he had even been even mildly attracted by her, he did not let it appear in his manner.

But one thing jarred.

"My goodness, Paul, how smart Pike's collar is!" Isabella had said. "Did you ever! You extravagant boy! It is good enough for a lady's bracelet. You had better give it to me! It will make the finest wedding gift I'll have!"

But Paul had snatched Pike up, the blood burning in his cheeks, and had laughed awkwardly and turned the conversation.

No one's fingers but his own were ever allowed to touch the sacred gold. ,

About this time his mother began to have the idea he ought really to marry. His father had been thirty at the time of his wedding with herself, and she had always thought that was starting too late. Twenty-three was a good age, and a sweet, gentle wife of Paul's would be the joy of her declining years—to say nothing of several grandchildren. But when this matter was broached to him first, Paul laughed, and when it became a daily subject of conversation, he almost lost that quick temper of his, which was not quite yet under perfect control.

"I tell you what it is, mother," he said, "if you tease me like this I shall go away on a voyage round the world!"

So the Lady Henrietta subsided into pained silence, and sulked with her adored son for more than a day.

"Paul is so unaccountably changed since his visit abroad," she said to her husband plaintively. "I sometimes wonder, Charles, if we really know all the people he met."

And Sir Charles had replied, "Nonsense! Henrietta—the lad is a man now, and immensely improved ; do leave him in peace/*

But when he was alone the father had smiled to himself—rather sadly—for he saw a good deal with his shrewd eyes, though he said no words of sympathy to his son. He knew that Paul was suffering still, perhaps as keenly as ever, and he honoured his determination to keep it all from view.

So the old year died, and the new one came— and soon February would be here. Ah! with what passionate anxiety the end of that month was awaited by Paul, only his own heart knew.

CHAPTER XXV

THE days passed on, March had almost come, and Paul heard nothing*. His father noticed the daily look of strain, and his mother anxiously inquired if he were dull, and if he would not like her to have some people to stay, and thus divert him in some fashion. And Paul had answered with what grace he could.

An intense temptation came over him to read all the Court news. He longed to pick up the ladies' papers he saw in his mother's sitting-room; such journals, he knew, delighted to publish the doings of royal lives. But the stem self-control which now he practised in all the ruling of his life prevented him. No, he had promised never to investigate—and neither in the letter, nor the spirit, would he break his word, whatever the suffering. The news, when it came, must be from his beloved one direct.

But ob! the unrest of these Hours. Ha3 tKek

hope come true?—and how was she? The days passed in a gnawing anxiety. He was so restless he could hardly fix his attention on anything. It required the whole of his will to keep him taking in the sense of the Parliamentary books which were now his study. The constant query would raise its head between each page—"What news of my Queen ?—what news of my Queen ?"

Each mail as it came in made his heart beat, and often his hand trembled as he lifted his pile' of letters. But no sight of her writing gladdened his eyes, until he began to be like the sea and its tides, rising twice a day in a rushing hope with the posts, and sinking again in disappointment.

He grew to look haggard, and his father's heart ached for him in silence. At length one morning, when he had almost trained himself not to glance at his correspondence, which came as he was dawdling over an early breakfast, his eye caught a foreign-looking letter lying on the top. It was no hand he knew—but something told him it contained a message—from his Queen.

He dominated himself; he would not even look at the postmark until he was away up in his own room. No eye but Pike's must see his joy —or

sorrow and disappointment. And so the letter burnt in his pocket until his sanctum was reached, and then with agonised impatience he opened the envelope.

Within was another of the familiar paper he knew, and ah! thank God, addressed in pencil in his lady's own hand. Inside it contained an enclosure, but the sheet was blank. With wildly beating heart and trembling fingers Paul undid the smaller packet's folded ends. And there the morning sunbeams fell on a tiny curl of hair, of that peculiar nondescript shade of infant fairness which later would turn to gold. It was less than an inch long, and of the fineness of down, while in tender care it had been tied with a thread of blue silk.

Written on the paper underneath were the words:

"Beloved, he is so strong and fair, thy son, bom the 19th of February."

For a moment Paul closed his eyes, and as once before a choir of seraphims were singing in his ears.

Then he looked at this minute lock again, and touched it with his forefinger. The strangest emotion he had ever known quivered through his being—the concentrated sensation of what he used to feel when his lady had spoken of their hope—a weird, tremulous, physical thrill. The dear small curl of hair! The actual, tangible proof of his own living son. He lifted it with the greatest reverence to his lips, and a mist of joy swam in his blue eyes. Ah! it was all too wonderful—too divine the thought! The essence of their great love—this child of his and hers. His and hers! Yes, their hope had not deceived them. It was true! It was true!

Then his mind rose in passionate worship of his lady. His goddess and Queen—the mainspring of his watch of life—the supreme and absolute mistress of his heart and soul. Never had he more madly desired and loved her than this day. He kissed and kissed her words in deep devotion.

But how and where was she?—was she well? ■—was she ill? Had she been suffering? Oh! that he could fly to her. More than ever the ter-riUe gall of their separation came to bim. It was.

his right, by every law of nature, to now be by her side.

But she was well—she must be well, or she would have said, and surely he soon would see her.

It was like a voice from heaven, her little written words, bridging the impossible—drawing him back to the knowledge and certainty that she was there, for him to love, and one day to go to. Fate could never be so unjust as to part him from—the mother of his child.

And then a state of mad ecstasy came over Paul with that vision; he could not stay in the house; he must go out under God's sky, and let his soul-thoughts fly into space. Dazzling pictures came to him; surely the spring was in his heart breaking through the frozen ground like a single golden crocus he saw at his feet—surely, surely the sun of life would shine again, and living he should see her.

He strode away. Pike gambolling beside him, and racing ahead and back again, seeming to understand and participate in his master's inward joy.

Paul hardly noticed where he went, his

thoughts exalting him so that he did not even heed to choose his favourite haunt, the wood against the sky-Hne. It was as if great blocks of icy fear and anguish were melting in the warmth. Hope and glory shone on his path, almost blinding him.

He left the park far behind, and struck away across the moor. As he passed some gipsy vans a swarthy young woman looked out, an infant in her arms, and gave him a smiling greeting. But Paul stopped and said good-day, tossing her a sovereign with laughing, cheery words—for her little child—and so passed on, his ^ad face radiant as the mom.

But the woman called after him in gratitude:

"Blessings on your honour. Your own will grace a throne."

And the strange coincidence of her prophecy set fresh thrills of delight bounding in Paul's veins.

He walked and walked, stopping to lunch at an inn miles away. He could not bear even to see his parents—or the familiar scenes at home; and as once before he had felt in his grief—^he and his joy must be alone to-day.

THREE WEEKS

When he turned to come back in the late afternoon, the torrent of his wild happiness had crystallised itself into coherent thought and question. Surely she would send him some more words and make some plan to see him. But at least he was in touch with her again and knew she was his own—his own. The silence had broken, and human ingenuity would find some way of meeting.

The postmark was Vienna—though that meant nothing at all; she could have sent Dmitry there to post the letter. But at best, even if it were Russia, a few days' journey only separated him from his darling and—his son! Then the realisation of that proud fact of parenthood came over him again. He said the words aloud, "My son!"

And with a cry of wild exaltation he vaulted a gate like a schoolboy and ran along the path. Pike bounding in the air in frantic sympathy. Thus Paul returned to his home again, hope singing in his heart.

But even his father did not guess why that night at dinner he raised his champagne glass and drank a silent toast—his eyes gazing into distance as if he there saw heaven.

CHAPTER XXVI

OF course as the days went by tHe sparkle of Paul's joy subsided. An infinite unrest took its place—a continual mad desire for further news. Supposing she were ill, his darling one? Many times a day he read her words; the pencil writing was certainly feeble and shaky—supposing— But he refused to face any terrible picture. The letter had come on the 26. of March; his son had been eleven days old then —two days and a half to Vienna—that brought it to eight when the letter was posted—and from whence had it come there? If he allowed two days more, say—she must have written it only five or six days after the baby's birth.

Paul knew very little about such things, though he understood vaguely that a woman might possibly be very ill even after then. But surely, if so, Anna or Dmitry would have told him on their own initiative. This thought comforted him a

THREE WEEKS

little, but still anxiety—^like a sleuth-Houn3—^pursued his every moment. He would not leave home—London saw him not even for a day. Some word might come in his absence, some message or summons to go to her, and he would not chance being out of its reach. More than ever all their three weeks of happiness was lived over again—every word she had said had sunk for ever in his memory. And away in his solitary walks, or his rides home from hunting in the dusk of the afternoon, he let them echo in his heart.

But the desire to be near her was growing an obsession.

Some days when a wild gallop had made his blood run, triumphant thoughts of his son would come to him. How he should love to teach him to sit a horse in days to come, to ride to hounds, and shoot, and be an English gentleman. Oh! why was she a Queen, his loved one, and far away —why not here, and his wife, whom he could cover with devotion and honour? Surely that would be enough for them both— z life of trust and love and sweetness; but even if it were not— there was the world to choose from, if only they were together.

THREE WEEKS

fTEe two—Paul and his father—^were a silent pair for the most part, as they jogged along the lanes on their-.way back from hunting.

One afternoon, when this sense of parenthood was strong upon Paul, he went in to tea in his mother's sitting-room. And as he leant upon the mantelpiece, his tall, splendid figure in its scarlet coat outlined against the bright blaze, his eye took in—^perhaps for the first time—^the immense number of portraits of himself which decorated this apartment—himself in every stage, from infantile days upward, through the toy rocking-horse period to the real dog companion—in Eton collars and Fourth of June hats—in cricketing flannels and Oxford Bullingdon groups—and then not so many, until one taken last year. How young it looked and smiling! There was one particular miniature of him in the holy of holiest positions in the centre of the writing-table —a real work of art, well painted on ivory. It was mounted in a frame of fine pearls, and engraved with the name and date at the back:

"Paul Verdayne—aged five years and three months."

It was a full-lengtfi picture of him standing

next a great chair, in a blue velvet suit and a lace turn-over collar, while curls of brightest gold fell rippling to his neck—rather short bunchy curls which evidently would not be repressed.

"Was I ever like that, mother?" he said.

And the Lady Henrietta, only too enchanted to expand upon this enthralling subject, launched forth on a full description.

Like it! Of course! Only much more beautiful. No child had ever had such golden curls, or such eyes or eye-lashes! No child had ever, in fact, been able to compare with him in any way, or ever would! The Lady Henrietta's delicate shell-tinted cheeks flushed rose with joy at the recollection.

"Darling mother," said Paul, as he kissed her, "how you loved me. And how cold I have often been. Forgive me—"

Then he was silent while she fondled him in peace, his thoughts turning as ever to his lady. She, too, probably, would be foolish, and tender, and sweet over her son—and how his mother would love her grandchild. Oh! how cruel, how cruel was fate!

Then he asked: "Mother, Hoes it take women

a long time to get well when they have children ? Ladies, I mean, who are finely nurtured? They generally get well, though, don't they—and it is quite simple—"

And the Lady Henrietta blushed as she answered:

"Oh! yes, quite simple—unless some complications occur. Of course there is always a faint danger, but then it is so well worth it. What a strange thing to ask, though, dear boy! Were you thinking of Cousin Agatha V*

"Cousin Agatha!" said Paul vaguely, and then recollected himself. "Oh, yes, of course—^how is she?"

But when he w^ent off to his room to change, his mother's words stayed with him—"unless some complications occur"—and the thought opened a fresh field of anxious wonderment.

At last it all seemed unbearable. A wild idea of rushing off to Vienna came to him—to rush there on the clue of a postmark—^but common sense put this aside. It might be the means of just missing some message. No, he must bear things and wait. This silence, perhaps, meant good news—and if by the end of April nothing

came, tKen he should have to break his promise and investigate.

About this time Captain Grigsby again came to stay with them. And the next day, as he and his host smoked their pipes while they walked up and down the sunny terrace, he took occasion to give forth this information:

"I say, Charles—I have located her—have you?"

"No! By Jove!" said Paul's father. "Hubert is away, you know, and I have just let the thing slide—"

"About the end of February did you notice the boy looking at all worried ?"

Sir Charles thought a moment.

"Yes—I recollect—d—d worried and restless —and he is again now."

"Ah! I thought so!" said Mark Grigsby, as though he could say a good deal more.

"Well, then—out with it, Grig," Sir Charles said impatiently.

And Captain Grigsby proceeded in his own style to weave together a chain of coincidences which bad struck him, until this final certainty.

THREE WEEKS

They were a clear set of arguments, and Paul's father was convinced, too.

"You see, Tompson told you in the beginning she was Russian," Captain Grigsby said after talking for some time, "and the rest was easy to find out. We're not here to judge the morals of the affair, Charles; you and I can only be thundering glad your grandson will sit on that throne all right."

He had read in one paper—^he proceeded to say —that a most difficult political situation had been avoided by the birth of this child, as there was no possible heir at all, and immense complications would ensue upon the death of the present ruler —the scurrilous rag even gave a resume of this ruler's dissolute life, and a broad hint that the child could in no case be his; but, as they pithily remarked, this added to the little prince's welcome in Ministerial circles, where the lady was greatly beloved and revered, and the King had only been put upon his tottering throne, and kept there, by the fact of being her husband. The paper added, the King had taken the chief par' in the rejoicings over the heir, so there was noth ing to be said. There were hints also of his mad

THREE WEEKS

fits of debauchery and drunkenness, and a suppressed tale of how in one of them he had strangled a keeper, and had often threatened the Queen's life. Her brother, however, was with her now, and would see Russian supremacy was not upset.

"Husband seems a likely character to hobnob with, don't he, Charles ? No wonder she turned her eye on Paul, eh ?" Mark Grigsby ended with.

But Sir Charles answered not, his thoughts were full of his son.

All the forces of nature and emotion seemed to be drawing him away from peaceful England towards a hornets' nest, and he—^his father— would be powerless to prevent it

CHAPTER XXVII

APRIL'S days were lengthening out in showers and sunshine and cold east wind. Easter and a huge party had come and gone at Verdayne Place, and the Lady Henrietta had had her hopes once more blighted by noticing Paul's indomitable indifference to all the pretty girls.

He was going to stand for Parliament in the autumn, when their very old member should retire, and he made that an excuse for his isolation; he was working too hard for social functions, he said. But in reality life was growing more than he could bear.

Captain Grigsby had sold the old Blue Heather and bought a new steam yacht of seven hundred tons—large enough to take him round the world, he said—and he had had her put in commission for the Mediterranean, and she was waiting for him tiow at Marseilles. Would Paul join him

for a trip? he asked, and Paul Hesitated for a moment.

If no news came by Friday—this was a Monday—then he should go to London and deliberately find out his lady's name and kingdom. In that case to cruise in those waters might suit his book passing well.

So he asked for a few days' grace, and Captain Grigsby gave a friendly growl in reply, and thus it was settled. By Saturday he was to give his answer.

Tuesday passed, and Wednesday, and on Thursday a telegram came for Paul which drove him mad with joy. It was short and to the point: "Meet Dmitr\'7d^ in Paris." Then followed an address. By rushing things he could just catch the night boat.

He went to his father's room, where Sir Charles was discussing affairs with his land steward. The man retired.

"Father," said Paul, "I am going immediately to Paris. I have not even time to v/ait and see my mother—she is out driving, I hear. Will you understand, father, and make it all right with her?"

And Sir Charles said, as he wrung his son's hand:

"Take care of yourself, Paul—I understand, my boy—^and remember, Grig and I are with you to the bone. Wire if you want us—and let me have your news."

So they had parted without fuss, deep feeling in their hearts.

Paul had telegraphed to the address given, for Dmitry, that he would be in Paris, and at what hotel, by the following morning. He chose a large caravanserai as being more suitable to unremarked comings and goings, should Dmitry's visit be anything of a secret one. And with intense impatience he awaited the faithful servant's visit.

He was eating his early breakfast in his sitting-room when the old man appeared. In all the journey Paul had not allowed himself any speculation—he would see and know soon, that was enough. But he felt inclined to grind this silver-haired retainer's hand with joy as he made his respectful obeisance.

"The Excellency was well?"

"Yes." And now for his news.

Madame had bid him come and see the Excti-lency here in Paris, as not being so inaccessible as England—and first, Yes, Madame was well— There was something in his voice as he said this which made Paul exclaim and question him closely, but he would only repeat that—^Yes, his lady was well—a little delicate still, but well— and the never-sufficiently-to^be-beloved son was well, too, his lady had told him to assure the Excellency—and was the portrait of his most illustrious father. And the old man lowered his eyes, while Paul looked out of the window, and thrilled all over. Circumstances made things very difficult for Madame to leave the southern country where she was at present, but she had a very strong desire to see the Excellency again—if such meeting could be managed.

He paused, and Paul exclaimed that o£ course it could be managed, and he could start that night.

But Dmitry shook his head. That would be impossible, he said. Much planning would be needed first. A yacht must be taken, and not until the end of May would it be safe for the

Excellency to journey south. At that time Madame would be in a chateau on the seacoast,

THREE WEEKS

and if the Excellency in his cruise could be within sight, he might possibly land at a suitable moment and see her for a few hours.

Paul thought of Captain Grigsby.

**I will come in a yacht, whenever I may," he said to Dmitry.

So they began to settle details. Paul imagined from Dmitry continuing to call his Queen plain "Madame" that she still wished to preserve her incognito, so, madly as he desired to know, he would wait until he saw her face to face, and then ask to be released from his promise. The time had come when he could bear the mystery no longer, but he would not question Dmitry. All his force was turned to extracting every detail of his darling's health and well-being from the old servant, and in his guarded, respectful manner he answered all he could.

His lady had indeed been very ill, Paul gathered—at death's door. Ah! this was terrible to hear—but lately she was mending rapidly, only she had been too ill to plan or make any arrangements to see him. How all this made his heart ache! Something had told him his passionate anxiety had not been without cause. Dmitry

THREE WEEKS

continued: Madame's life was not a Kappy one, the Excellency must know, and the difficulties surrounding her had become formidable once or twice. However, the brother of Madame was with her now, and had been made guardian of her son—so things were peaceful and the cause of all her trouble would not dare to menace further.

For once Dmitry had let himself go, as he spoke, and a passionate hate appeared in his quiet eyes. The "Trouble" was of so impossible a viciousness that only the nobility and goodness of Madame had prevented his assassination numbers of times. He was hated, he said, hated and loathed; his life—^spent in continual drunkenness, and worse, unspeakable wickedness—was not worth a day^s purchase, but for her. The son of Madame would be loved forever, for her sake, so the Excellency need not fear for that, and Madame's brother was there, and would see all was well.

Then Paul asked Dmitry If his lady had been aware that he had been ill in Venice. And he heard that. Yes, indeed, she had kept herself informed of all his movements, and had even sent Vasili back on learning of his danger, and was

THREE WEEKS

on the point of throwing all prudence to the winds and returning herself. Oh! Madame had greatly-suffered in the past year—the old man said, but she was more beautiful than ever, and of the gentleness of an angel, taking continuous pleasure in her little son—indeed, Anna had said this was her only joy, to caress the illustrious infant and call him Paul—such name he had been christened —after a great-uncle. And again Dmitry lowered his eyes, and again Paul looked out of the window and thrilled.

Paul! She had called him Paul, their son. It touched him to the heart. Oh! the mad longing to see her! Must he wait a whole month ? Yes —Dmitry said there was no use his coming before the 28th of May, for reasons which he could not explain connected with the to-be-hated Troublesome one.

Every detail was then arranged, and Dmitry was to send Paul maps, and a chart, and the exact description and name of the place where the yacht was to lie. The whole thing would take some time, even if they were to depart to-morrow.

"The yacht is at Marseilles now," Paul said, "and we shall start on the cruise next week.

Let
me have every last instruction poste restante, at Constantinople—and for God's sake send me news to Naples on the way."

Dmitry promised everything, and then as he made his obeisance to go, he slipped a letter into Paul's hand. Madame had bidden him give the Excellency this when they had talked and all was settled. He would leave again that night, and his present address would find him till six o'clock if the Excellency had aught to send in return.

And then he backed out with deep bows, and Paul stood there, clasping his letter, a sudden spring of wild joy in his heart.

And what a letter it was! The very soul of his loved one expressed in her own quaint words.

First she told him that now she expected he knew who she was, and as they were to meet again—which in the beginning she feared might never be—all reason for her incognito was over. Then she told him—to make sure he knew—^her name and kingdom. "But, sweetheart," she added, "remember this—^my proudest titles ever are to be thy Loved one, and the Mother of thy son." Here Paul kissed the words, madly thrilling with pride and worship. She spoke of her still un-
3ying love, and of her anguishing sorrow all the winter at their separation, and at length the joy of their little one's arrival.

"Thy image, my Paul! English and beautiful, as I said he would be—not black and white like me. And oh! beloved, thou must always increase thy knowledge of statesmancraft to help me to train him well."

Then she made a glorious picture of their child's future, and Paul lay back in his chair and closed his eyes—^the brightness of it all dazzled him—while his heart flew to her in passionate adoration. She went on to speak of their possible meeting. Her villa was but two hundred yards from the sea, only he must follow exactly all Dmitry's instructions, or there might be danger for them both; but at all costs she could not live much longer without seeing her lover.

"Thou art more than a lover now, my Paul— and I am more than ever Thine."

Thus it ended. And Paul spent most of the rest of his day reading and re-reading it, and writing his worshipping answer.

By night both he and Dmitry had started on their homeward journeys.

CHAPTER XXVIII

THE Lady Henrietta was desolated when Paul and his father announced their intention of taking a month or six weeks'" cruise with Captain Grigsby. So unnecessary, she said, at this time of the year, almost the beginning of May, when England was really getting most enjoyable. And they were obliged to pacify her as best they could.

The Mediterranean! Such miles off—and so eccentric, too, starting when other people would be leaving! Really, she had never ceased regretting ever having tolerated her son's travels the year before. Since then there had been no certainty in any of his movements.

"Darling mother," said Paul, "I must see the world."

And Sir Charles had snorted and chuckled, as was his habit.
So they sailed away from Marseilles, this party of three, like a gunboat under sealed orders. A cruise to the Greek Isles, and beyond, was what they said attracted them. "Especially

the beyond !" Captain Grigsby had added, with a grunt to Sir Charles. And if the ardour of love and impatience boiled in Paul's veins, the spirit of interested adventure animated his old friend and his parent.

They had not spoken much on the subject to the young man. He had briefly asked Mark Grigsby to do him this service to take him to a far sea in the new Blue Heather, and there to land him when he should give the word.

May was a fair month, and an adventure is an adventure all the world over, so Mark Grigsby had given a joyful assent.

Then Sir Charles had suggested accompanying them, and was welcomed by the other two as a third for their party with extra pleasure.

"I shall grow a young man again before I have done. Grig!" he had said happily. But down in his heart lurked some undefined fear for Paul, and that was the real reason for his journey.

THREE WEEKS

They had a pleasant voyage, and picked up ktlers at Naples, which only added to Paul's'im-'paHence to be there. But they were not to arrive before the end of May, so the Grecian Archi-^f^elago could be investigated.

Life in these sunny seas was a joy to all con-.lerned, and Paul's eyes—illuminated by his lady's ever-present spirit—saw beauties and felt shades and balances of which his companions never dreamed. So they came at last to the Bosphorus and Constantinople.

Here full instructions awaited them. That night Paul took his father and his friend some w^ay into his confidence, as he showed them the chart and read aloud the directions. On the 29th of May, should the weather prove favourable, they were to anchor towards night at a certain spot—latitude and longitude given—^and when they heard a sea-bird cry sharply three times, Paul was to come ashore to where he would see a green light. Vasili would be waiting for him, and from there it was but a few steps to the garden gate of the villa by the sea, in which his lady was passing the summer. It all seemed perfectly simple—only, the directions added, he must leave

THREE WEEKS

again before dawn, and the yacht be out of sight before daylight, as complications had occurred since the letter to Naples, and the To-be-hated one had not left the capital, so things were not so easy to manage, or safe.

Paul's impatience knew no bounds. The concentrated pent-up longing of all these months was animating him. To see his lady again! To clasp her! To kiss her—to kneel to her—and give her homage and worship. And to behold his little son. Always he carried the minute flaxen curl in a locket, and often he had looked at it, and tried to picture the wee head from which it had been cut. But she—his love—would bring his son to him—and perhaps let him hold him in his arms. Ah! he shut his eyes and imagined the tender scene. World she be changed? Should he see the traces of suffering? But he would caress all memory of pain away, and surely this meeting would only be the forerunner of others to come. Fate could never intend such deep, true love as theirs to be apart. An exaltation uplifted him. And if his lady were a Queen, and wore a crown, he felt himself the greatest king on earth, for was not he the absolute ruler

THREE WEEKS

of her heart? And who could wish for a more glorious kingdom?

The hours from Constantinople seemed longer than the whole voyage. He could hardly keep his attention to talk coherently about ordinary things at meals, and his father and Mark

Grigsby left him practically alone.

At last, at last, the 29th of May dawned, boiling hot and cloudlessly fair.

For obvious reasons they stayed beyond sight of the coast until darkness fell, and then came close inshore. It was a starlit night, with not a breath of air, and no moon would illuminate their whereabouts.

Paul dressed with the greatest care; never had he been more particular over his toilet. Tompson found him exigeant!

He had broadened and filled out in the past year, and his fair face was tanned, and blooming with health and excitement.

"The best-looking young devil a woman's eye could light on!" Mark Grigsby said, as he and Sir Charles watched him descend the gangway to the boat, when the impatiently awaited signal had been given.

THREE WEEKS

i<t

'God keep him safe, Grig," was all Sir Charles coiild mutter, with a grunt in his throat.

The maddest excitement was racing through Paul, as he held the tiller-ropes and made straight for the light. And once he felt in his pocket to assure himself he had not forgotten Dmitry's pistol, which he had cleaned and loaded himself that afternoon.

He knew this adventure might be a dangerous one, simple as it looked superficially, and now he was an expert revolver shot, thanks to constant practice.

The light proved to be in a little sheltered cove, with a small landing-stage. And—yes— the man who held it was the Kalmuck, Vasili.

"Welcome, welcome to the Siyafelstvo/' he whispered, as he kissed Paul's hand. And then in perfect silence they began to ascend a path. Presently it stopped abruptly. They had come up perhaps not fifty feet, when their way was barred by a great nail-studded door.

"Hist!" said Vasili softly, and instantly it was opened from within, and Dmitry peered anxiously at them.

"Ah, the saints be blessed, the Excellency is

THREE WEEKS

safe," he said. But they must not delay a minute, he added. The Excellency must return to the waiting boat! A slight but unexpected ill-fortune had befallen them, connected with the to-be-execrated Troublesome one, and it would not be safe for the Imperial Highness if the Excellency should land to-night. She had sent him to say that the Excellency was to keep out at sea for two days, and return steaming past, and if he saw a white flag flying from the villa roof, then at night he was to anchor and come ashore at this same time. If not, for the moment he must go on back to Constantinople, where news and further instructions would be sent him.

As he spoke Dmitry indicated the return path', and bid the Excellency follow him, and hasten, hasten. This was a terrible blow to Paul, but the thought that he might bring danger to his beloved one made him not hesitate a moment.

They descended the path in silence, and as he stepped into the boat the old servant whispered, the Imperial Highness had bid him assure the iSxcellency that all was well, the meeting was 'Only deferred, when they should have several ilays together in ^fety. "The saints protect the

THREE WEEKS'

Excellency/' the faithful creature added. Then, when Paul was safely in the boat, he stood back to make sharply three times the sea-bird's cry.

The weird minor notes floating out on the night seemed a wailing echo of the agonised disappointment in Paul's heart—more than once a mad impulse to go back convulsed his being before he reached the yacht—but it was not till afterwards that he remembered as a strange circumstance the fact that with Dmitry's first words at the nail-studded door Vasili had vanished into darkness.

CHAPTER XXIX

THE two days out at sea were a raging impatience to Paul, in which he learnt to understand all the torments of Tantalus. To know and feel her near, and yet not to be allowed to get to her! It was an impossible cruelty.

The two grey-headed men's hearts ached for him, and Captain Grigsby delivered himself of this aphorism:

"Say what you will, Charles, but youth pays the devil of a long price for its pleasures. Here you and I snored like a couple of porpoises all last night, while the boy paced the deck and cursed everything."

And Sir Charles had only grunted, for he was feeling very deeply for his son.

There was a fresh breeze blowing when the time was up and they sighted land again, and long

THREE WEEKS

before any possible shore could be examined, Paul stood—his strongest glasses in his hand—on the look-out.

At length they came in full view, and alas! there could be no mistake, the flagstaff upon the villa roof was empty.

To the day of his death Paul will keep a vivid picture of the pure white-columned house. No semi-Oriental architecture met his view, but a beautiful marble structure in the graceful Ionic style, seeming a suitable habitation for his Queen.

It was approached by groves of ilex, from a wall at the edge of the sea. And now Paul could discern the landing-stage, and the great studded door.

A sensation of foreboding—a wild, mad anxiety, filled his being. What had happened? Why might he not land ? Then for the first time that fact of Vasili's vanishment came into his min-d. Was there something sinister in it? Had he scented any danger to his Queen, and gone to see? A whirlwind of questions and frenzied speculation shook Paul's brain. But there was nothing to be done now but to cram on all steam and make for Constantinople.

THREE WEEKS

He looked again. The green jalousies were lowered over the windows, all seemed peaceful, silent and deserted. No living being wandered in the gardens. It might have been a mausoleum. for the dead. And as this thought came to him Paul almost cried aloud.

Then he dominated himself. How weak and intolerably foolish to imagine evil where perhaps none was! Why should his thoughts fly to terrible reasons for the postponement of his joy, when in truth they could as well be of the simplest? A sudden call to the city—^a descent of some undesirable spying eye—a hundred and one possible things, all much more likely than any ones of fear.

He would not permit another moment of won-^ der. He would regain his calm and wait like a man for certainty. Thus his face wore an iron mask and his thoughts an iron band. And presently they came to Constantinople.

But of what followed afterwards it is difficult to write. For fate struck Paul on that warm June morning, and blasted his life, so that for many days he only saw red, and lived in hell.

THREE WEEKS

Every one knows the story which at the time convulsed Europe. How a certain evil-living King, after a wild orgie of mad drunkenness, rode out with two boon companions to the villa of his Queen, and there, forcing an entrance, ran a dagger through her heart before her faithful servants could protect her. And most people were glad, too, that this brute paid the penalty of his crime by his own death—his worthless life choked out of him by the Queen's devoted Kalmuck groom.

But only Paul and his father, and Mark Grigsby, know the details, which were told in Dmitry's heart-bxclvcn letter. How that night, the 29th of May, at the hour the Excellency was expected, he—Dmitry—was waiting in the garden to meet him and conduct him through the gloom, when, while he stood there under the stars, the Imperial Highness had called him softly, telling him to take the message down to the Excellency, which he did. How he had never dreamed that immediate danger threatened her, or that the King was there, or he would not have left her for any peril to the Excellency, who was

THREE WEEKS

after all a man and could fight. And how Vaslli, being younger and more quick of wit, had suspected, hearing his message as he gave it to the Excellency, that all was not well, and had hastened to the house—too late to save his Queen.

And then the faithful servant took up Anna's tale. How this good girl had been watching on the side of the villa towards the town, and had heard the King come battering at the gate. How she had flown to warn her mistress, but that the hnperatorskoye had sent her back to watch, saying she herself would call Dmitry to protect them. Of course—as they now guessed—on purposethat Anna should not hear her message to him—as the Queen knew full well if he—Dmitry—heard from Anna the King was there, and she—the Queen—in danger, he would not leave her, even to do her bidding. Then of how the King had thrust the frightened servants aside, and strode with threats and oaths into the hall, accompanied J)y his two vile men. And how Anna had implored the Queen to hide while there was yet time. But how that shining one had stood only listening intently for the sea-bird's cry, and then when she heard it, had turned in triumph to the entering King, saying to Anna that nothing mattered now the Excellency was safe!

On her face, as she looked at this monster, was no dread of death, or aught but scorn and fearless pride. How Anna, seeing the dagger, had screamed, and tried to get between, but had been seized by one of the execrated men, and there been forced to watch the murder of her worshipped Queen. Ah! that had been a moment the saints could never efface! The splendid lady had stood quite still, her head thrown back, while this hound of hell had lurched towards her—hissing through his evil teeth this dreadful sentence: "Since thou hast at last obeyed me and found me an heir, making the people love me, I have no more use for thee. It will be a joy to kill thee!"

And with that he had plunged the dagger in her heart.

Of all that followed the Excellency would know. How Vasili had entered, scattering the minions like a mad bull, and springing upon the villainous King, had torn his life out on the marble floor.

iTHus ended the letter.

Ah, God! For Paul had come the tears. But for her—cold steel and blood. And so, as ever, the woman paid the price.

CHAPTER XXX

NOW some of you who read will think her death was just, because she was not a moral woman. But others will hold with Paul she was the noblest lady who ever wore a crown. And in all cases she is beyond our puny reasonings.

But her work in Paul's heart still lives, and will live to the end of his life. Although for long months after the agony of that June day, nothing but hate and passion and misery had the ruling of him.

He could not bear his kind. His father and Captain Grigsby had left the yacht to him and let him cruise alone. But who can know of the hideous, ghastly hours that Paul spent then, ever obsessed with this one bitter thought ? Why had he not gone back? Why had he not gone back when that impulse had seized him? Why had

Vasili, an3 not lie, Had tfie satisfaction of killing this vile slayer of his Queen ?

Even the remembrance of his child did not rouse him. It was safe with the Grand Duke Peter—a king at four months old! But what of sons, or kings, or countries—nothing could make up for the loss of his Queen! And to think that she had died to save him! Save him from what ? A brush with three besotted drunkards, whom it would have been great joy to kill 1

There were moments when Paul went mad with passion, and lay and writhed in his berth. So long months passed, and at last he dominated himself enough to come back to his home.

And if the Lady Henrietta had exclaimed that he appeared ill before on his return, she was dumb now with sorrow at the change. For Paul had looked upon Medusa's head of horror, and, as well as his heart, his face seemed turned to stone. He was gentle with his mother, and let her caress him as much as she would, but nothing any one could say could move him—even Pike's joyous greeting.

The whole of God's world was his enemy—for was he not alone there, robbed of his mate ? Presentty the reaction from this violence came, and an intense apathy set in. A saltless, tasteless existence. What was Parliament to him? What was his country or his nation? or even his home? Only the hunting when it came gave him some relief, and then if the run were fast enough, or the jumps prodigiously high, or his horses sufficiently fresh to be difficult, his blood ran again for a brief space. But beyond this life was hell, and often he was tempted to use that little pistol of Dmitry's, and end it, and sleep. Only the inherent manly English spirit in him, deep down somewhere, prevented him.

All this time his father grieved and grieved, and the Lady Henrietta spent hours in tears and prayer. Sir Charles had told her their son had met with a great sorrow, and they must bow their heads and leave him in peace, so there were no more gay young parties at Verdayne Place, and gone for ever were the visions of the grandchildren. Only Mark Grigsby was a constant visitor, but then—^he knew.

Thus a year passed away, and Paul left on a voyage round the world. An Englishman's stern duty to be a man at all costs was calling him at

THREE WEEKS

last—bidding him in change of scene to try and overcome the paralysing dominion of his grief. But as far as that went the experiment proved futile. If moments came when circumstances did divert him, such as one or two great storms he happened to come across, and one or two exciting situations—still, when things were fair and peaceful, back would rush the ever-living ache. That passionate void and loss for which there seems no remedy.

Gentle, pleasant women longed to lavish worship upon him, and Paul talked and was polite, but all their sweetness touched him no more than summer ripples stir the bottom of a lake. He seemed impervious to any human influence, though when the look of a mountain or the colour of beech-trees would remind him of the Biirgen-stock ?vnguish as fresh as ever stabbed his heart. Yet all this while, unknown to himself, his faculties were developing. He read deeply. He had unconsciously grown to apply his darling's lucid reasoning to every detail of his judgment of life. It was as if it had before been written in cypher for him, and she had now given him the key. His mind was untiring in its efforts to master

THREE WEEKS

subjects, as his splendid physique seemed tireless in all manner of sport.

Thus he saw the world and its peoples, and was an honoured guest among the great ones of the earth. But the hardness of adamant was in him. He had no beliefs—no ambitions. He dissected everything with all the pitiless certainty of a sur-geon^s cold knife. And if his life contained an aim at all, it was to get through with it and find oblivion in eternal sleep.

Thoughts of his little son would sometimes come to him, but when they did he thrust them back, and shut his heart up in a casing of ice.

To feel—was to suffer! That perhaps was his only creed; that and a blind, sullen rage against fate. This was the lesson his suffering had taught him, and they were weary years before he knew another side.

The first time he saw a tiger in India was one of the landmarks in the history of his inner emotions. He had gone to shoot the beasts with a well-known Rajah, and it had chanced he came upon a magnificent creature at very close quarters and had shot it on sight. But when it lay dead, its wonderful body gracefully moving no

THREE WEEKS

more, a sickening regret came over Faul. Of all things in creation none reminded him so forcibly of his lost worshipped Queen. In a flash came back to him the first day she had lain on the skin which had been his gift. Out of the jungle her eyes seemed to gleam. In his ears rang her words, "I know all your feelings and your passions. And now I have your skin—for the joy of my skin." Yes, she had loved tigers, and been in sympathy with them always, and here was one whose joy of life he had ended!

No, he could never kill one more. After this expedition for weeks he was restless—^the incident seemed to have pierced through his carefully cultivated calm. For days and days, fresh as in the first hours of his grief, came an infinite sensation of pain—just hideous personal pain.

So time, and his journeys, went on. But no country and no change of scene could dull Paul's sense of loss, and the great vast terrible finality of all hope.

The hackneyed phrase would continually ring in his brain of—Never again—never again! Ah! God! it was true he would hold his beloved one— never again. And often unavailing rebellion

THREE WEEKS

against destiny would rise up in him, and he would almost go mad and see red once more. Then he would rush away from civilisation out into the wild.

But these violent emotions were always followed by a heavy, numb lethargy until some echo or resemblance roused him to suffering again. The scent of tuberoses caused him anguish unspeakable. One night in New York he was obh'ged to leave the opera because a woman he was with wore some in her dress.

Thus, with all his strong will, there were times when he could not control himself or his grief.

He had been absent from England for over two years, when the news came to him far out in America of his Uncle Hubert's death. So he had gone to join the world of spirits in the vast beyond ! Paul did not care! His only feeling was one of relief. No more fear of hearing, perhaps, some chance idle word. But he remembered his mother had loved her handsome brother, and he wrote a tender letter home.

Then something in the Lady Henrietta's answer touched him vaguely and decided him to return. After all—^because life was a black barren waste

THREE WEEKS

to him—what right had he to dim all joy in the two who had given him being? Yes, he would go back, and try to pick up the threads anew.

There were great quiet rejoicings in his parents' hearts at their son's third homecoming. And like a wild beast tamed for a time to perform tricks in a circus, Paul conformed to the ordinary routine. The question of his entering Parliament was mooted again, but this he put aside. As yet he could face no ties. He would do his best by staying at home most of the year—but when that call of anguish was upon him, he must be free once more to roam.

Then hope began to bloom in the Lady Henrietta's heart as flowers after rain. Surely this great unknown grief was passing—surely her adored one would settle down again.

CHAPTER XXXI

BUT the months went by without healing Paul's grief. Time only coated it with a dull, callous crust. He had got into a hard way of taking everything as it came. He did not fly from society, or ape the manners of the misanthrope; he went to London, and stayed about and played the game. But all with a stony, bald indifference which made people wonder.

No faintest inkling of his story had ever leaked out. And it seemed an incomprehensible attitude towards life for a young and fortunate man. Those who had looked for great things from his birthday speech shook their heads sadly at the unfulfilment.

So time passed on, until one day at the beginning of February, nearly five years after the light had gone out of his life, a circumstance happened which proved a turning-point of great magnitude.

It was quite a small thing—just the brutalised hardness in a gipsy woman's face!

The sun was setting that late afternoon when he strode home across the moor with Pike, and they came upon some gipsy vans. Paul looked up—it was no unaccustomed sight, only they happened to be in exactly the same spot where the like had stood that morning long ago, when in his exuberant happiness at the news of his little son's birth he had tossed the young woman the sovereign.

The door of the last van was open, and there, sitting on the steps in an attitude of dull sullen idleness, was the same swarthy lass, only now she was altered sadly! No more the proud young mother met his view, but a hard, gaunt, evil-looking woman.

She knew him instantly, and her black eyei fiercened; as he came up close to her she said without any greeting:

"I lost him, your honour—him and my Bill in the same blasted year, and I ain't never had no other."

Paul stopped and peered into her brown face in the fading light.

"So we have been both through hell since then, my poor girl?" he said.

The gipsy woman laughed with bitter harshness as she echoed back the one word *'Hell!'"— and afterwards she added with a wail: "Yes,

they're dead! and there won't be never no meet-

• if mgr

; And Paul went on—but her face haunted him.

Was there the same hard change in himself, he wondered? Was he, too, brutalised and branded with the five years of hell? Surely if so he had gone on a lower road than his darling would have had him travel.

Then out of the mist of the dying day came the memory of her noble face as it had been in that happy hour when they had floated out to the lagoon, and she had told him—her eyes alight with the feu sacre —her wishes for his future.

But what had he done to carry them out—those lofty wishes? Surely nothing. For, obsessed with his own selfish anguish, he had lived on with no single worthy aim, with no aim at all except to forget and deaden his suffering.

Forget! Ah God! that could never be. For had she not said there was an eternal marriage ^S6

of their souls—in life or in death they could never be parted ?

And he had tried to break this sacred tender bond, when he should have cherished every memory to comfort his deep pain v^ith its sweetness. What had he done ? Let sorrow sink him to the level of the poor gipsy girl, instead of trying to do some fine thing as a tribute to his lady's noble teaching.

He strode on in the dusk towards his home, his thoughts lashing him with shame and remorse.

And that night, when he and Pike were alone in- his own panelled room, he broke the seal of those beautiful letters w^hich, with directions for them to be buried with his body at his death, had lain in a packet hidden away from sight all these years, freighted with agonised memory.

He read them over carefully, from the first brief note to the last long cry of love which Dmitry had brought him to Paris. Then he lay back in his chair, while his strong frame shook with sobs, and his eyes were blinded by scorching, bitter tears.

But suddenly it seemed as if his lady's spirit

THREE WEEKS

stood beside him in the firelight's flickering gleam, whispering words of hope, pleading to come back from the cold grave to his heart, there to abide and comfort him.

He heard her golden voice once more, and it fell like soft, healing rain, so that he stretched out his arms, and cried aloud:

"My darling, beloved one, forgive me for these five wasted years—sweetheart, come back to me never to part again. Come back to my heart, and dwell there. Angel Queen!"

Then, as the days went on, all the world altered for him. Instead of the terrible bitterness against fate which had ruled his heart, a new tenderness grew there. It seemed now as though he were never alone, but lived in her ever-present memory. And with this golden change came thoughts of his child—that little life neglected for so long. What had he done? What cruel, terrible thing had he done in his selfish pain ?

Each year Dmitry had sent him a letter of news, and each year that day had held ghastly hours for him in the reopening of old anguish—> the missive to be read and quickly thrust out of

THREE WEEKS

sight, the thought of it to be strangled and fof-^' gotten.

And now the little one would soon be five years old, and his father's living eyes had never seen him! But this should no more be so, and he wrote at once to Dmitry.

By return of post came the answer. The Excellency indeed would be welcome. The Regent —^the Grand Duke Peter—had bidden him say that if the Excellency should be travelling for pleasure, as the nobility of his country often did, he would gladly be received by the Regent, who was himself a great chasseur and voyageur. The Excellency would then see the never-to-be-sufficiently-beloved baby King. Of this glorious child he—Dmitry—found it difficult to write. It was as if the Imperatorskoye breathed again in his spirit, while he was the portrait of his illustrious father, proving how deeply and well the Imperatorskoye must have loved that father. If the Excellency could arrive in time for the Majesty's fifth birthday, on the 19th of February, there was to be a special ceremony in the great church which the Regent thought might be of interest to the Excellencjr.

THREE WEEKS

Paul wired back he would travel night and day to be in time, and he instructed Dmitry to have the necessary arrangements made that he might go straight to the church, in case unforeseen delay should not permit him to arrive until that morning.

It was in a shaft of sunlfght from the great altar window that Paul first saw his son. The tiny upright figure in its blue velvet suit, heavily trimmed with sable, standing there proudly. A fair, rosy-cheeked, golden-haired English child— the living reality of that miniature painted on ivory and framed in fine pearls, which made the holy of holies on Lady Henrietta's writing-table.

And as he gazed at his little son, while the organ pealed out a Te Deum and the sweet choir sang, a great rush of tenderness filled PauFs heart, and melted forever the icebergs of grief and pain.

And as he knelt there, watching their child, it seemed as if his darling stood beside him, telling him that he must look up and thank God, too— for in her spirit's constant love, and this

glory of their son, he would one day find rest and consolation.
THE END

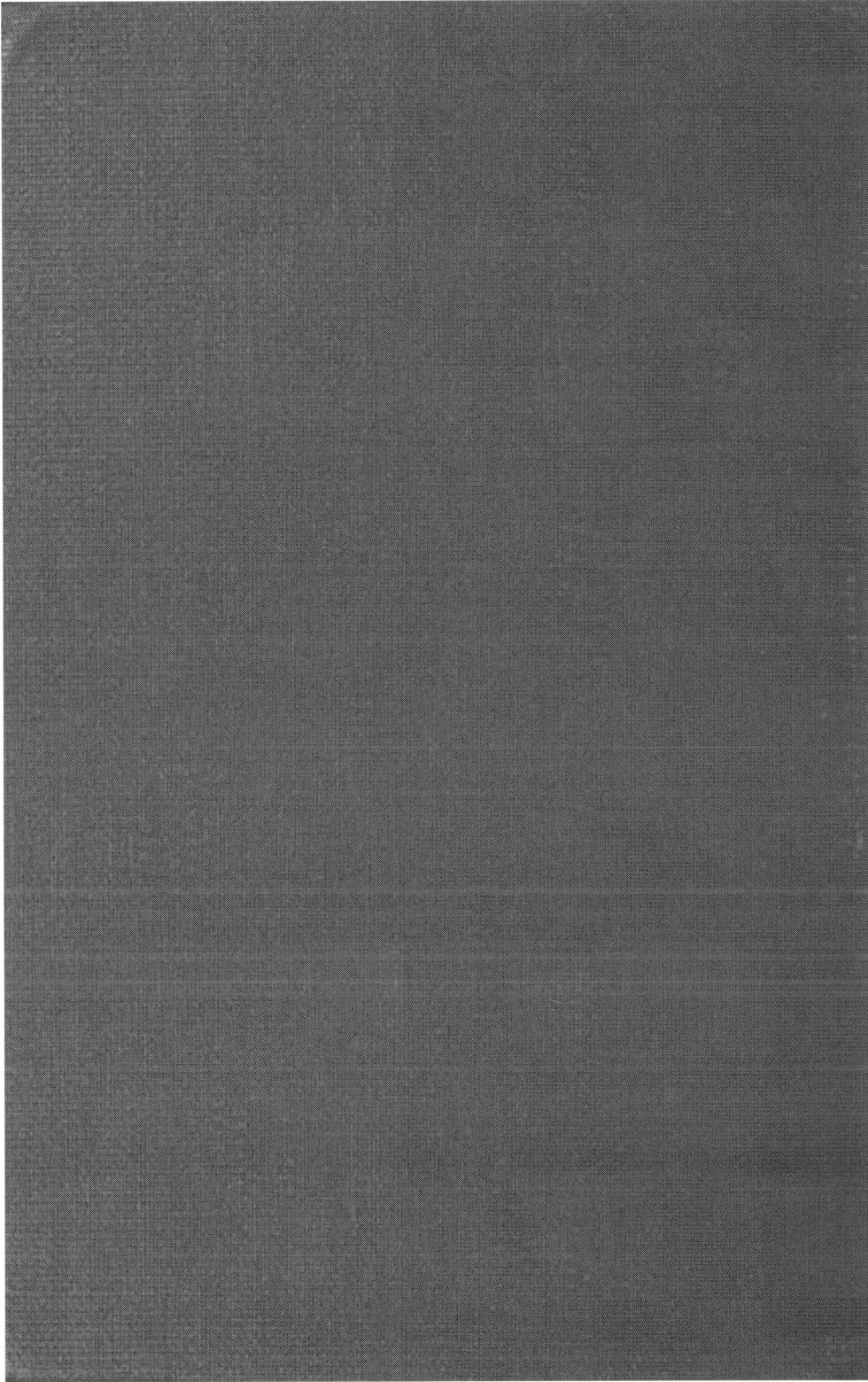

Printed in Great Britain
by Amazon